The Mystery
of Dead Man's Curve

Laura E. Williams

SCHOLASTIC INC.

New York Toronto London Auckland Sydney
Mexico City New Delhi Hong Kong

This book is dedicated to all
of Mrs. Henneberry's students—
past, present, and future

A Roundtable Press Book

For Roundtable Press, Inc.:
Directors: Julie Merberg, Marsha Melnick, Susan E. Meyer
Project Editors: Betsy Gould, Meredith Wolf Schizer
Editorial Assistant: Carrie Glidden
Designer: Elissa Stein
Illustrator: Laura Maestro

ISBN 0-439-21725-3 JMYST

12 11 10 9 8 7 6 5 4 3 2 1 0   1 2 3 4 5/0

Printed in the U.S.A.
First Scholastic printing, September 2000

Contents

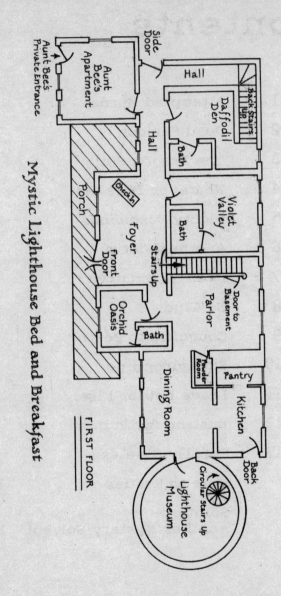

Mystic Lighthouse Bed and Breakfast

FIRST FLOOR

Side Door

Aunt Bee's Private Entrance

Aunt Bee's Apartment

Hall

Back Stairs Up

Daffodil Den

Bath

Hall

Check In

Foyer

Front Door

Porch

Violet Valley

Bath

Stairs Up

Orchid Oasis

Bath

Parlor

Door to Basement

Dining Room

Powder Room

Pantry

Kitchen

Back Door

Circular Stairs Up

Lighthouse Museum

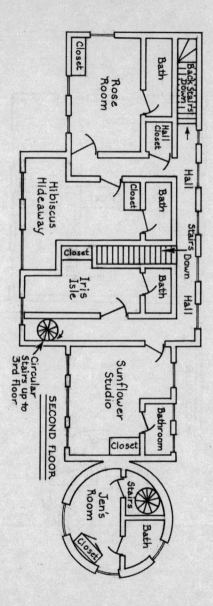

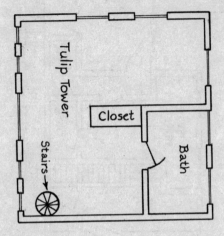

Tulip Tower

Closet

Bath

Stairs →

THIRD FLOOR

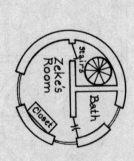

Zeke's Room

Stairs

Bath

Closet

Note to Reader

Welcome to *The Mystery of Dead Man's Curve*, where YOU solve the mystery. As you read, look for clues pointing to the guilty person. There is a blank suspect sheet in the back of this book. You can copy it to keep track of the clues you find throughout the story. These are the same suspect sheets that Jen and Zeke will use later in the story when they try to solve the mystery. Can you solve *The Mystery of Dead Man's Curve* before they can?

Good luck!

1
Attempted
· Murder

"They'll be here any minute," Aunt Bee called out as she pulled at her flowing skirt to make sure it was hanging straight. She eyed the foyer to double-check that everything was in place and nervously fussed with the flowers sitting on the front desk.

Jen looked over at her twin brother, Zeke, and they both grinned. Even though the Mystic Lighthouse Bed and Breakfast had been open for two years, Aunt Bee still got nervous before new guests arrived.

"Don't worry," Jen teased, tugging on her aunt's long gray braid. "Zeke and I cleaned all the rooms that will be used, put full toilet paper rolls in the bathrooms, and even washed the windows. Everything is ready."

Bee straightened the registration book on the desk for the third time. "Did you change the sheets?"

Jen gasped. "Oh, no, we forgot the beds!"

Zeke tried to hide his smile. "The beds! How will our guests sleep tonight?"

Aunt Bee scowled as she lunged playfully at her niece and nephew. Jen laughed and expertly ducked out of Aunt Bee's reach, but Zeke wasn't as quick. Their aunt caught him and gave him a big bear hug before letting him go with a giant kiss on the cheek.

Zeke wiped it away with pretended disgust. He always thought it was funny that his aunt got so nervous about guests arriving. After all, she had run the B&B since it opened. With the twins' help, of course. Jen and Zeke had moved in with their aunt Bee and uncle Cliff nine years ago, after their parents died. That was when the twins were just two-year-old toddlers. Their uncle Cliff passed away just before the B&B's grand opening. Aunt Bee was the only family member Jen and Zeke had left. Even though they called her Aunt Bee, she was more like a mother to them. Or a grandmother, actually, because she was really their grandma Estelle's sister.

Slinky, their Maine coon cat, jumped down from a high cabinet and swished her fluffy tail back and forth. With a long meow, she stepped on top of Woofer, their Old English sheepdog. Woofer, asleep as usual, opened one lazy eye, then quickly closed it.

He was used to Slinky walking on him and obviously didn't want to interrupt his nap to shake her off. Aunt Bee and the twins laughed.

"As you know," Aunt Bee said, quickly getting back to business, "the five guests we're having this week are all candidates for the principal's job at Mystic Middle School. So you two had better be on your best behavior."

"Aren't we always?" Jen asked with a mischievous little smile.

"Most of the time," Aunt Bee admitted. "But not always. Besides, don't you want to make a good impression on your new principal?"

"I guess so," Jen agreed.

"Of course," Zeke said.

Aunt Bee smiled at them. "Good. Now let's do one more sweep in here."

Zeke looked at the hardwood floors that already glowed with polish. He supposed it wouldn't hurt to sweep the corners of the foyer. "I'll go get the broom," he offered.

Jen eyed the floor. "It doesn't look dirty to me. I just mopped it yesterday."

Aunt Bee adjusted the curtains. "A little sweeping won't kill you."

Jen groaned. "It might."

"Sometimes I can't believe you and Zeke are twins," Aunt Bee said, laughing. "You look the same, with your dark wavy hair and bright blue eyes, but why is he so neat and you're so not?"

"He's one minute older than me," Jen said with a grin. "That makes him more responsible."

Zeke returned from the kitchen with the broom and dustpan and started to sweep the corners of the room. Jen couldn't see a speck of dust, but Zeke kept sweeping as if there were piles of dirt. He bent over and poked the broom under the cabinet. When he pulled out the broom, a dust ball filled with cat hair came along with it.

"Good job mopping yesterday," Zeke teased his twin, a sparkle lighting up his blue eyes.

Jen shrugged. "Oops." She moved closer to the mess. "Hey, what's that?" Gingerly, she tugged on a string that was snaking out from under the cabinet. When she pulled, her neon-green yo-yo rolled out. "Jeez, this has been missing for weeks!" she exclaimed. "How did it get under there?"

"It's that rascal Slinky," Aunt Bee said from the other side of the foyer where she was plumping the floral cushions on each overstuffed chair. "She'll steal anything she can get her paws on."

Using the Mystic, Maine, T-shirt she was wearing,

Jen rubbed the dust and hair off her yo-yo.

Aunt Bee looked at her with one eyebrow raised. "That was a nice clean shirt," she said. "Before you used it as a dust rag, that is."

Jen looked down. Sure enough, she looked as if she had been swept out from under the cabinet along with her yo-yo.

As Zeke pushed the hairy pile into a dustpan and headed for the kitchen, Jen raced through the dining room and into the lighthouse tower. Aunt Bee and Uncle Cliff had renovated the circular building so that she and Zeke could each have a bedroom in the tower. Jen's room was on the second floor; Zeke's was on the third. Both of their rooms were curved on one side with awesome views of the Atlantic Ocean and the bay just to the south.

Jen dashed through the Lighthouse Museum of Memorabilia that she and Zeke had set up on the first floor of the tower, then ran up one flight of circular stairs to her room. She flung open her door. The twins had helped Aunt Bee decorate all the guest rooms with flower themes, but Jen had decorated her own room, so instead of flowery wallpaper, posters of every possible sport covered her walls. Her favorite was a shot of two huge men who looked like sumo wrestlers playing tiddledywinks. Zeke's room, on the other hand, always made her laugh because it looked like a set from *Star Wars*.

Catching her breath, Jen put on a clean T-shirt. She threw her dusty shirt onto the pile of dirty clothes on the floor of her closet. She'd take them to the basement laundry room later, she decided as she shoved the closet doors shut and charged back downstairs.

Zeke was helping Aunt Bee refold one of the homemade quilts they kept draped over the backs of chairs and couches around the B&B. Suddenly he stopped folding and cocked his head. "Someone's coming."

Jen didn't hear anything, but she ran to the front door and threw it wide open. The cool, salty air blew in along with the sound of the Atlantic Ocean crashing against the rocky beach just below the bluff. It was rather warm for Maine at this time of year, but she wasn't complaining.

Sure enough, a small green car pulled up the circular driveway. A very tall woman with frizzy orange hair unfolded herself from the car. Her wide, freckled face looked upset.

Zeke hurried down the stairs to help her with her luggage, but the woman had already grabbed her suitcase from the trunk of the car and slammed it shut before Zeke reached her.

"I'll carry that for you," he offered.

"Oh, thank you," the woman said, handing over her suitcase with a shaking hand. "I'm Mrs. Adams." She reached into her car and snatched up her purse, along with a new toothbrush and box of toothpaste.

Aunt Bee stepped forward. "I'm Beatrice Dale, but please call me Bee. Come in and relax. Did you have a long trip?"

Jen moved out of the way as everyone walked into the foyer. She looked at Zeke struggling with the suitcase. Jen smiled because she knew exactly what Zeke was thinking. *Next time you get to carry the suitcase!* It wasn't uncommon for their thoughts to mix together. They often found themselves thinking the same thing. It was almost like *hearing* each other's thoughts.

Zeke and Jen caught up with their aunt and Mrs. Adams at the check-in desk.

They got there just in time to hear Mrs. Adams say, "And then it happened."

"What happened?" Aunt Bee asked as she wrote Mrs. Adams's name in the registry.

"Someone tried to kill me!"

2
Dead
Serious

"Wow!" Jen exclaimed just as Zeke asked, "How?"

"Look at my hands. They're still trembling."

The three of them looked. Sure enough, her hands were shaking.

"I'll get you some tea," Aunt Bee offered as she led Mrs. Adams to a chair. She went into the kitchen to heat some water.

"How did it happen?" Zeke asked.

"There's a terrible turn in the road along the coast, just before you get here—"

"That's called Dead Man's Curve," Jen interrupted.

The woman shuddered, and Zeke glared at his sister. Mrs. Adams was obviously upset enough without Jen adding to it. Sometimes Jen opened her mouth without thinking.

"And so, what happened?" he prodded gently.

Mrs. Adams took a deep, steadying breath. "Well, right before that curve is a little market called Quick Stop or something. I needed to stop there to get a couple of items I forgot." She motioned to the toothpaste and toothbrush still sitting on the check-in counter where she'd left them. "I was very careful pulling out of the parking lot. But as soon as I got to the first part of that dangerous curve, another car—a bright red car—hit me from behind. I skidded off the road and onto the tiny shoulder. I could have smashed through the guardrail, sailed over the cliff, and crashed down on the jagged rocks below."

"How awful!" Aunt Bee exclaimed, returning with a mug of cinnamon tea for the guest. "Were you hurt?"

"No, thank goodness," Mrs. Adams said as she gratefully clasped the steaming mug. "But my taillight was broken."

"I'm sure it was just an accident," Aunt Bee said.

"Then why didn't the other driver stop?" Mrs. Adams demanded. She shook her head, sending her orange hair bouncing back and forth. "No, that driver meant to hit me and leave me for dead. I'm sure of it."

Mrs. Adams sipped her tea. "Luckily, I was able to get back on the road and drive here. And to top everything off, I cut my finger. It probably happened when I got out to check my taillight." She held up the index finger of her right hand, which she'd wrapped in tissue.

At a nod from her aunt, Jen hurried to the powder room by the parlor to get Mrs. Adams a bandage.

"You should fill out a police report," Aunt Bee suggested, reaching for the phone that sat on one side of the front desk.

"Oh, no," Mrs. Adams protested. "I don't want to do that."

"But if you do," Zeke said, "the police might be able to find out who hit you."

"You could have been killed," Jen added, handing the bandage to Mrs. Adams. She shrugged when her brother and aunt glared at her.

"No, no," Mrs. Adams said. "I don't want to start off in this town with a complaint to the police, especially if I'm worthy enough to get the job." She sat up straighter. "We'll just try to forget this little incident ever happened. Everything will be fine." She smiled, but Zeke noticed her lips trembled. Mrs. Adams was obviously still upset, but he had to give her credit for being so brave.

"If you're sure," Aunt Bee said doubtfully. "Just let me know if you change your mind."

With that, Zeke carried her suitcase down the hall to her first-floor room while Mrs. Adams followed.

"You're in the Daffodil Den," he told her.

"What on earth does that mean?" she asked. But as soon as Zeke opened the door to her room, she breathed a sigh of appreciation.

Zeke grinned. Guests were always impressed by the rooms. Each one was decorated in a different flower theme. He thought the decorations were a bit overwhelming, but Aunt Bee loved her flowers and wanted everyone else to enjoy them, too.

"I just adore daffodils," Mrs. Adams gushed, surveying the room. "And look at that wonderful mobile."

Zeke glanced at the mobile of hanging ceramic daffodils. "One of the shops in town sells mobiles with everything from flowers to whales," he explained. "You'll have to check it out."

Mrs. Adams smiled and reached into her purse. "I certainly will. Thank you so much for your help."

Zeke returned to the foyer to tell Aunt Bee and Jen that Mrs. Adams was going to lie down and relax a bit before dinner. Then he flashed a dollar bill at Jen as Aunt Bee took the empty mug back to the kitchen.

She narrowed her eyes at him. It was always a contest to see who could get more tips.

Zeke tucked the bill into his pocket. "Do you think Mrs. Adams's car was hit by accident?"

"Why would someone purposely run her off the road?" Jen asked.

Instead of answering, Zeke pointed. "Look, Mrs. Adams forgot her toothbrush and toothpaste. I'd better bring them to her."

"I'll do it," Jen offered, but Zeke had already picked up the items.

"Forget it," Zeke said with a grin. "She's not going to tip you just for bringing these to her."

As Zeke walked down the hall he said over his shoulder, "The least they could have done was given her a bag for this stuff."

"It's better for the environment not to get a bag," she called after him, but he was too far away to hear her.

As Jen turned around, the front door banged open and a large bearded man stomped in. Jen hurried forward to take his suitcase, but he wouldn't let go of it.

"Hello," he announced in a hearty voice. "I'm Dr. Bowles."

Jen tried to take his suitcase a second time, but he pulled it out of her reach.

"I'll take care of this," he said. Although Dr. Bowles smiled when he talked, Jen could see he was dead serious. A shiver of unease tickled her spine.

"Now, that's strange," Dr. Bowles said as he walked over to the check-in desk and Aunt Bee hurried to stand behind it. "I know I had my wallet when I left." He patted his pockets several times and finally found it in the inside pocket of his jacket. He shook his head. "Ever since my wife died five years ago, I keep losing everything. She used to say if she wasn't around, I'd forget to screw my head on straight in the morning." He burst out laughing. "At least I didn't forget my head today!"

Jen glanced at Zeke, who had just come back from his delivery. *Okayyyy*, they both thought as they started to laugh. It was hard not to when Dr. Bowles was chuckling louder than a department store Santa Claus. He looked a little bit like one, too, with a big belly and a full salt-and-pepper beard. But even as she laughed, Jen couldn't forget the look he had given her when she had tried to carry his bag. *There's something weird about this guy*, she thought.

Just then, two more people entered the B&B. One was a thin man with slightly hunched shoulders and thinning brown hair who introduced himself as Mr. Crane. He clutched a well-worn briefcase with one clawlike hand. The other guest, a woman who introduced herself as Ms. Hartlet, wore a navy blue suit and a shy smile. She'd pulled her dark brown hair into a tight bun at the back of her head.

"I've heard of you," Dr. Bowles said to Mr. Crane.

"You're the principal at Kennedy Middle School in Lake Cove, Michigan. I've read all about your award-winning programs. You're doing a great job."

Zeke couldn't believe it when the thin man didn't even say thank you. He simply scowled at them all and shook his head as though he didn't like compliments. Zeke saw his sister was about to say something, but he jumped in before she could put her foot in her mouth.

"Would you like me to show you to your room, Mr. Crane?" Zeke asked. "You're on the second floor in the Hibiscus Hideaway."

The man rubbed his long pointed nose and said, "Fine."

They left, and a few minutes later, Jen led Ms. Hartlet upstairs to the Rose Room, and Aunt Bee pointed Dr. Bowles to the Violet Valley, right off the foyer.

"Oh, this is lovely," Ms. Hartlet said when Jen opened her door. "How pretty and cozy. I'm sure I'll be very comfortable." She handed Jen a crisp dollar bill.

Jen nodded her thanks. When she got downstairs, she nearly ran into her brother. She waved her tip in front of his nose.

"Boy, Mr. Crane never smiles," Zeke grumbled. "I don't think he's too happy about being here." He held up a quarter. "And he's not a big tipper."

"Jen? Zeke?" Aunt Bee called from the front desk.

The twins hurried over. In the foyer they saw a young man wearing a jogging suit and running shoes, surrounded by piles of luggage. Jen groaned inwardly and felt the same vibes from her brother. So much to carry. Ugh. No tip was worth it.

"Mr. Mitchell will be staying in the Orchid Oasis," Aunt Bee said, much to Jen's and Zeke's relief.

As the twins lugged his bags into the room closest to the entry foyer, Mr. Mitchell directed them. "Careful with that one," he ordered as Jen nearly broke her back trying to pick up one of the suitcases. "It's very important."

Zeke picked up a large bag that turned out to be rather light. He couldn't imagine what was in it, but he didn't think it would be polite to ask.

When they finally dragged the last bag into his room, Mr. Mitchell shut his door without even saying thank you. The twins flopped onto a pair of chairs.

"I'm glad the B&B isn't booked up this week; it looks like we'll have our hands full. I wonder what was in Mr. Mitchell's bags," Zeke said.

"I don't know," Jen said. "But it's pretty strange to have so much luggage for only five days."

"Hey, we've had weirder people than that stay here."

Jen laughed. "That's for sure! Remember the lady who brought all her pictures of her cats and insisted on showing them to everyone?"

"Over and over again," Zeke finished for her.

They both chuckled at the memory, then Zeke headed for his room. "I'm going to try out my new video game, the one with the snowboarders. Want to try it?"

Jen scrunched up her nose. "No, thanks. That game makes me dizzy. It's way too realistic. Anyway, I told Stacey I'd call her. We're going to kick around a soccer ball."

"Don't get beaned in the face," Zeke called over his shoulder as he took off.

"Don't fall off a mountain," Jen shouted back.

⤙⤚

Jen and Zeke didn't see any of the candidates again until dinner. Aunt Bee served the evening meal family style, with everyone sitting on either side of the long dining room table. She served breakfast every day, but on special occasions she also served dinner. Tonight she'd made her famous spaghetti with meat sauce and a Caesar salad. The twins had been in charge of making a large basket of garlic bread.

As Dr. Bowles handed Mrs. Adams the bread, she

shuddered. "That's quite a ring you're wearing!"

Zeke looked at the large gold ring wrapped around Dr. Bowles's plump pinky. It was a serpent with two red eyes. Zeke thought it was pretty cool looking.

Dr. Bowles laughed. "You don't like snakes?"

"I hate them," she answered.

"I don't like them, either," Ms. Hartlet said from across the table. "They give me the creeps."

Jen noticed Mr. Crane shudder.

"They're so slimy," Mrs. Adams said.

"Actually," Zeke said, "they're not slimy at all. They're quite dry to the touch."

Mrs. Adams shivered. "Well, I don't intend to touch one, so I'll just have to take your word for it."

As they were finishing dinner, Aunt Bee announced that she locked the doors at eleven each night. "If any of you are out after that, simply come to my private entrance, the blue door with the wreath on it, and knock. I'll let you in."

"I think I'll go for a stroll along the bluff," Dr. Bowles said, rubbing his large stomach as he popped a last bite of buttery bread into his mouth. "I want to work off some of this delicious dinner."

"Strolling isn't going to do you much good," Mr. Mitchell said. "Running is much better exercise. That's what I'm going to do. Anyone want to come?"

"Strolling sounds better to me," Mrs. Adams said.

"Me, too," said Ms. Hartlet. She turned to Mr. Crane. "Would you like to join us?"

Mr. Crane scowled. "I should think not. I'm going to prepare for my interviews. After all, only *one* of us can get this job."

The Dragon Box

Jen squinted at the red digital clock radio next to her bed. She groaned. It wasn't even midnight, but something had woken her up. Slinky lay curled up next to her, purring softly, so it couldn't have been the cat. Was Woofer barking? She listened intently, but all she could hear was the crash of waves outside her window.

A tingle of unease ran across her shoulders. Zeke and Aunt Bee made fun of how deeply she slept. She could usually sleep through thunderstorms or Slinky walking on top of her.

She silently slipped out of bed and tiptoed to the window. Outside, the bright moon illuminated the ocean, making it glow with a silvery light. The yard looked deserted. From the other side of the room, she could look back toward the bay, but if she opened her window and leaned out, she could also see the far side of the parking lot over the roof of the B&B.

She stuck her head out the bay-side window and was breathing in the cool misty air when she saw something move out of the corner of her eye. Was that a person moving around the parking lot, or was it just a midnight shadow? It seemed that the harder she stared, the less she could see.

Her breath caught in her throat. Yes! There was someone snooping at the far end of the lot. Well, maybe not snooping, she decided. It was hard to tell what the person was doing from so far away. But why would any-one be in the parking lot at this time of night? Aunt Bee had already locked the doors, so whoever it was either didn't belong anywhere near here, or was a guest who was locked out of the B&B.

The shadowy figure disappeared again. Just when Jen was deciding she must have dreamed the whole thing, the person stepped back into sight, right in the bright moonlight. This time she recognized the bulky figure. Dr. Bowles!

When he disappeared from sight again a few seconds later, he didn't reappear. Jen pondered this as she snuggled back into bed. Before she came to any conclusions, she fell fast asleep. And this time, nothing woke her until Zeke banged on her door at six the next morning.

Before Jen had a chance to tell Zeke about the midnight prowler, Mr. Crane stormed into the dining room where everyone was already eating the steaming-hot blueberry muffins that Aunt Bee had just set out in a basket on the dining table.

"Who stole my briefcase?" Mr. Crane demanded. His pinched face and the scalp showing through his hair were red with anger. "I had it last night, and this morning it's gone!"

"Could you have left it somewhere?" Aunt Bee asked, concern in her voice.

Mr. Crane's lips thinned. "Absolutely not! All my important notes were in my briefcase. I didn't let it out of my sight for one second! Someone stole it right out of my room, and I demand to know who it was."

Everyone looked at one another.

Jen stared at Dr. Bowles. Did he look guilty, or was it her imagination?

"How on earth could someone steal it out of your room?" Mr. Mitchell asked, taking a large bite of muffin. "We all have locks on our doors."

Mr. Crane's eyes shifted for a second. Jen glanced at Zeke. She knew what he was thinking: Mr. Crane had forgotten to lock his door.

Ms. Hartlet quietly asked, "Surely you locked your door last night?"

Mr. Crane didn't answer right away. Then he said, "Of course I did. I'm not a fool."

Zeke and Jen looked at each other again, positive he was lying. Even so, if someone had stolen his briefcase, something very suspicious was going on.

"I'm sure we'll find it," Aunt Bee said, passing him the butter. "Why don't you have a muffin to start your day?"

"How can I possibly eat with such a catastrophe at hand?" With that he made an about-face and stalked out of the dining room.

"The poor man," Ms. Hartlet said softly. "He seems so upset. But I'm sure he's overprepared for these interviews. I see it in my top students all the time. Even the littlest quiz puts them in a tizzy."

Zeke knew exactly what she meant. Tests and quizzes were very important if he wanted to keep his grades up. He knew Jen didn't worry about them half as much as he did, yet she seemed to get exactly the same marks. That didn't seem fair to him at all.

Jen nudged him on the shoulder. It was time to walk to the bus stop at the bottom of the hill.

When they got outside, Jen grinned at her brother. "Can you imagine getting bent out of shape over a quiz?"

"Very funny," he said, laughing. Jen loved to tease him about how much he studied.

"Just kidding," Jen said. "But Mr. Crane sure was upset about his briefcase. You'd think he had gold hidden in there instead of some dumb old notes."

Zeke shook his head. "I can't believe someone actually sneaked into his room and stole it."

That reminded Jen about seeing Dr. Bowles last night, and by the time the bus picked them up, she had told her brother the whole story.

"Maybe you dreamed the whole thing. Dr. Bowles doesn't seem like a thief to me," Zeke said, sitting across the aisle from Jen, who sat down next to her best friend.

Stacey leaned over, her bright blond hair curling around her face. "Who's a thief?"

Jen and Zeke looked at each other, silently deciding it wasn't such a good idea to tell Stacey that a possible future principal might be a thief. The whole school would know by lunch.

"Oh, nobody," Zeke said nonchalantly. "Just something we saw on television last night."

Stacey made a face at him. "Yeah, right. Like you two ever watch TV."

The three of them laughed, knowing she was right, but at least it changed the subject for the rest of the ride.

As Jen and Zeke walked through the front doors of Mystic Middle School with their friends, a loud voice boomed, "There they are! The bed-and-breakfast twins!"

Jen lowered her head, her cheeks flaming. "This is not happening. How did they get here before us, anyway?"

"They weren't in a slow yellow school bus," Zeke answered, trying not to move his lips. He knew how good teachers were at reading lips.

"Jen! Zeke! Over here."

They had no choice but to look up and wave to Dr. Bowles. Mrs. Adams and Ms. Hartlet waved, too. Mr. Mitchell was too busy straightening his tie. Zeke couldn't believe he was wearing a pair of blue-and-white running shoes with his gray suit. Scowling as usual, Mr. Crane looked severe in his black suit, white shirt, and dark blue tie. He stuffed his hands into his pockets as though he didn't know what to do with them without a briefcase to hang on to.

Someone dug Zeke in the ribs and said, "Principal's pet!"

Zeke grinned at his friend Tommy. "I can't help it if they're staying at our B&B and they happen to think Jen and I are adorable." Laughing, he and Tommy headed for their homeroom.

Jen tried to slip by the B&B guests, but Mrs.

Adams stopped her with a cheery smile. "How are you this morning, my dear?" Mrs. Adams trilled as she fluffed her brightly colored hair.

"Fine," Jen mumbled. She could feel the other kids staring at her. "And you?" This was one of those times when she wished Aunt Bee hadn't taught them to be so polite.

"Wonderful, thank you." She took a deep breath through her nose. "Something about this Maine air. It's so fresh and invigorating."

Jen smiled and nodded, though all she could smell was chalk dust. She said good-bye and hurried away. Stacey caught up with her.

"Who are they?" Stacey asked.

"They're all interviewing to be the next principal, and they're staying at the B&B."

Stacey giggled. "Lucky you."

"Yeah, right!"

~

After school, Aunt Bee greeted the twins with freshly baked chocolate chip cookies. They both had homework to do, but first they needed to tidy the guests' rooms. That was their main job at the B&B and neither of the twins minded doing it. It was fun to see how the way the guests kept their rooms reflected their personalities.

They always cleaned the rooms in the same order, starting downstairs with the Daffodil Den, going up the back stairs to clean the upstairs rooms, then coming down the front stairs to clean the remaining two guest rooms. This week that meant starting in Mrs. Adams's room and ending with Dr. Bowles's room.

Slinky slunk into the Daffodil Den with them. While the twins dusted, swept, and put out clean towels, the cat pounced, pranced, and pawed at all the loose, dangling items.

Mrs. Adams's clothes were hung neatly, Jen noticed as she shut the closet door. Her clothes were all bright shades of red, orange, and yellow—just as colorful as her hair. She and her belongings went well with the room's yellow trimmings.

Zeke read the title of the novel on her bedside table. It was called *Murder at the Library* by Esther Barrimore, and it looked as if it had never even been opened.

Mrs. Adams had obviously picked some wildflowers last night and put them in her drinking glass on the dresser. They looked very cheerful.

Jen chased Slinky out from under the bed, so they could move upstairs to Ms. Hartlet's room.

"Look," Zeke said. "She hardly unpacked." Two

almost identical-looking dark tailored suits hung in the closet. And one pair of dark low-heeled pumps stood primly on the closet floor.

"At least that keeps the room neat," Jen said, dusting the rosy pink windowsill. "Maybe she doesn't think she'll make it through all the interviews, so she doesn't want to get too comfortable."

"If that's the reason, she sure doesn't have much confidence in herself."

Jen moved on to dust the night table, where she noticed something was preventing the drawer from closing all the way. She opened the drawer an inch and discovered a pair of dark brown leather gloves. "How weird," she said, pointing. "Who wears gloves at this time of year?"

Zeke turned to her. "Hey, stop being so nosy. We'll never get finished at this rate."

With one last look at the gloves, Jen tucked them into the drawer and shut it all the way. Then she followed her brother out of the room.

Mr. Crane's room was also neat as a pin. Not a single thing was out of place. There were no shoes lying around, no loose ties, no books on the bedside table. Slinky jumped onto the dresser and knocked over the only personal possession Jen could see in the entire room.

Jen picked up the framed photo of a plump

woman with curly hair and a wide smile and set it gently back on the dresser.

"I like rooms like this," Zeke said as he shut the door and locked it behind them.

"That's just because you're a neat freak," Jen teased.

They went down the front stairs and opened the door to Mr. Mitchell's room. They were shocked at the sight of it.

"You should feel right at home in this mess," Zeke jeered, staring around with a mixture of disgust and amazement.

"Hey, even I'm not *this* bad," Jen retorted.

The floor was littered with jogging suits, sneakers, dumbbells, and an exercise mat. Magazines covered his unmade bed: *Sports Illustrated*, *Men's Health*, *Karate Magazine*, and many others. With a groan, they started stacking the magazines on the table by the window. After they had made the bed, they placed the dumbbells in a neat row against one wall and the shoes against another.

"He has *five* pairs of running shoes," Jen said, amazed.

When they finally finished, they heaved a sigh of relief and headed for the Violet Valley. As they walked down the hall, lugging their cleaning supplies, Mrs. Adams slipped out of Dr. Bowles's room, closing the door quietly behind her.

"Hi," Zeke said.

Mrs. Adams whirled around. "Oh, I didn't hear you coming."

"Did you need something?" Jen asked, trying not to sound suspicious.

"I just got back and thought I'd look around this lovely old house." She shrugged slightly. "Of course, as soon as I realized this was a guest room, I came out. I adore the way you've decorated each room in a different flower theme."

"Aunt Bee is in charge of the decorating," Jen said. She held up a bucket of cleaning supplies. "We're in charge of the cleaning."

Mrs. Adams laughed as she walked away. The twins let themselves into Dr. Bowles's room, relieved that he kept his room rather neat.

"Wow, look at this cool box," Jen exclaimed.

Zeke came closer to the dresser and stared at the wooden box, which had an intricately carved dragon on it. "This is strange," he said, pointing to the initials above the lock.

"M. C. R.," Jen read out loud. "Those aren't his initials—his last name is Bowles."

Suddenly, the twins heard a noise behind them. Dr. Bowles had stepped into the room and was staring openmouthed at the twins. He immediately snatched the box off the dresser. Zeke heard something inside it rattle.

Dr. Bowles glared at the twins. "Don't ever, ever touch that box again."

"We didn't touch it," Jen protested. "We only—"

But Dr. Bowles cut her short. "Just get out of here. If I ever catch you snooping around in here again, I'll tell your aunt!"

4
Whatever
It Takes

"Dr. Bowles is like Dr. Jekyll and Mr. Hyde," Jen said under her breath as they carried the cleaning supplies back to the kitchen pantry. "One minute he's Mister Jolly, and the next he's about to rip off our heads."

Zeke nodded. "There must be something important about that box. I heard rattling when he grabbed it."

"Maybe it's diamonds or something."

"Sure," Zeke said with a sarcastic edge to his voice. "Mr. Crane has gold in his briefcase and Dr. Bowles has diamonds in his box." He shook his head. "Where do you come up with these ideas anyway?"

Jen grinned. "Wait till you hear what I think about the others."

Zeke groaned. "I'm not sure I want to hear this." But when Jen didn't say anything, he added, "Okay, tell me."

Jen dropped the bucket in the corner of the pantry and leaned the broom against the wall. She turned to her twin and ticked off the guests on her fingers. "We've done Bowles and Crane. Then there's Adams and her frizzy orange hair that is too wild to be believed. I think it's really a wig and she's an undercover spy on a mission to catch Mr. Crane and Dr. Bowles."

Zeke rolled his eyes. "She's not exactly my idea of a secret agent."

"That's why she would be so perfect for the job. No one would suspect her. Mr. Mitchell is on the run from the police, which is why he wears running shoes all the time. He can make a quick getaway. And Ms. Hartlet is . . ." Her voice trailed off as she stared at the ceiling, thinking.

"Don't tell me you haven't figured her out yet," Zeke said as they settled at the kitchen table with some drinks.

Jen sipped on her tall glass of lemonade, then leaned forward and lowered her voice. "Ms. Hartlet is probably the most dangerous of them all because she seems so innocent."

"You're nuts," Zeke said, waving his glass of milk and nearly sloshing half of it on the table.

Jen shrugged and sat back casually. "Maybe, maybe not."

Once the guests had left for their dinner with the superintendent of schools, Jen and Zeke sat down with Aunt Bee in the kitchen. When it was just the three of them, they ate at the small round table in the cozy kitchen.

The kitchen was one of Jen's favorite rooms. Aunt Bee collected all sorts of bee knickknacks. She had covered the fridge with bee magnets and hung bee-patterned curtains at the kitchen window. There were also bee-shaped pot holders and cushions, bee figurines, and bee note cards. Postcards featuring bees that her friends had sent her were taped to the cabinets. Aunt Bee even had a hive-shaped telephone with a large bee for the hand piece.

Jen liked to tease her aunt by saying the kitchen was *bee-eautiful*.

"Why are you so tired tonight?" Zeke asked his aunt as he scraped the last bit of chocolate cream pie off his plate. "You've been yawning all through dinner."

"I didn't get much sleep last night," Aunt Bee admitted, getting up to do the dishes. "Dr. Bowles knocked on my door at eleven-forty-five. I can't imagine what he was doing out so late, but he said he simply lost track of the time out on the bluff."

Jen looked at her brother and lifted her eyebrows. So she hadn't been dreaming after all.

"That's weird," Zeke said.

Aunt Bee shrugged. "I did stay up awhile wondering about it, which is why I'm so tired today."

"We'll take the garbage out for you," Zeke said.

"We will?" Jen countered.

Zeke gave her a "just do it" stare.

The twins each picked up a large black bag stuffed with garbage and headed outside to the bins they kept on the parking lot side of the B&B.

Slinky wound between Zeke's feet as he walked, almost tripping him. "Scoot!" he said, but the cat ignored him and gave his ankles one last rub before prancing ahead of them. She made it to the garbage bins before them, and by the time they'd caught up, she'd found something to play with.

Zeke hefted his bag over the top of a bin and Jen did the same.

They stood for a moment laughing at Slinky, who tumbled and pounced at a scrap of red plastic.

"You'd think it was a mouse, the way she's enjoying herself," Zeke commented. "Where did she get that piece of broken plastic anyway?"

"Beats me." Jen lunged for the cat, but Slinky

playfully darted away, the plastic piece clamped between her sharp little teeth.

As they were returning to the back entrance of the B&B, Zeke said, "I wonder what Dr. Bowles was doing last night—"

Jen grabbed his arm, her mind no longer on Dr. Bowles. "Look!" She pointed to one of the parked cars. The guests had gone to dinner in two cars, leaving three behind. "That red car. It has a bashed-in front fender!"

In the fading daylight, they hurried over to the car and crouched in front of it, examining the damage. The fender was crumpled and red paint had chipped off in places, leaving rusty brown marks.

"I'll bet it was this car that almost ran Mrs. Adams over the cliff!"

Zeke agreed. "But whose is it?"

The twins raced inside to check the registration cards Aunt Bee kept behind the check-in desk.

"Here it is," Zeke said.

Jen read over his shoulder. "Mr. Mitchell!"

They heard footsteps and voices on the front porch and quickly put away the metal file box.

The twins watched Mr. Mitchell enter the B&B, tugging on his tie to loosen it. Jen nudged her brother in the ribs and whispered, "Do you think he tried to run Mrs. Adams off the road?"

As though Mr. Mitchell had heard her, he stared back at the twins with narrowed eyes. Jen gave him a small smile and waved. Mr. Mitchell didn't wave or smile back.

When he turned away from them, Zeke said softly, "He sure looks guilty."

Just then, Dr. Bowles burst through the front door holding a briefcase over his head. "I've found it!" he shouted.

Mr. Crane whirled around. "That's my briefcase!" He lunged forward. "Where was it?" he demanded as Dr. Bowles handed it over.

"Just next to the porch in those bushes. I saw the cat duck in there, and when I looked closer, there it was. The cat was sitting on it."

"Slinky found the briefcase?" Jen asked.

Dr. Bowles nodded. "Looked that way to me."

"That's ridiculous," Mr. Crane nearly spat out. "And I suppose you're going to tell me that the cat put it there, too." With one hand he held up the case, and with the other he twirled the numbered lock and opened it. He quickly rifled through the papers, looked satisfied, and closed the briefcase with a sharp click.

"It's a relief that you have it back," Aunt Bee said.

Mr. Crane opened his mouth as though he was

going to say something, but the tinkle of piano keys coming from the parlor cut him off. The twins followed the sound with the other guests.

Mrs. Adams sat on the piano bench, humming as she played. Aunt Bee kept the old upright piano tuned, even though Jen and Zeke had stopped taking lessons last year.

"Let's sing some songs," Mrs. Adams suggested, her fingers running gracefully across the keys despite the bandage on her right forefinger.

The twins looked at each other. *Songs? Did Mrs. Adams think this was camp?*

"Not for me," Mr. Crane said stiffly. "I have work to do." He shook his briefcase for emphasis.

Dr. Bowles laughed. "Oh, stay, it'll do you good to relax. Don't be a hermit."

Mr. Crane frowned, but he stayed, sitting stiffly on a side chair.

Jen and Zeke shared a seat in the corner where they had a good view of the room—especially of Mr. Mitchell.

Aunt Bee entered the parlor and walked over to Ms. Hartlet. "This came in the mail for you today."

Ms. Hartlet took the letter with a surprised "Thank you."

As Mrs. Adams began to play "Michael, Row Your Boat Ashore," Jen watched Ms. Hartlet. She looked worried as she opened the envelope and unfolded a letter.

Even from across the room, Jen could see Ms. Hartlet heave a heavy sigh as she read it. Then she started to sing halfheartedly as she absently shredded the letter.

After three songs, Mr. Crane stood up abruptly and stomped out of the room, hugging his briefcase to his chest as though he was afraid someone would snatch it from him.

Soon the other guests trickled out of the room as well. Before she left, Ms. Hartlet gathered up the slips of paper that she had torn.

Only Jen, Zeke, and Aunt Bee remained.

Aunt Bee yawned. "I'm going to lock up early tonight since everyone is already in. And then I'm going to bed!" She looked at her watch. "It's time for you two to hit the sack, too."

"We will," Zeke said as their aunt left the room. Then he turned to Jen. "Did you see him do anything suspicious?"

"Who?"

Zeke groaned. "Mr. Mitchell. Remember?"

"I remember," Jen said defensively. "I just forgot

for a second. Anyway, I didn't see him do or say anything suspicious. Did you?"

Zeke shook his head and stood up to leave.

"I'm just going to look for Slinky," Jen said. She liked to take Slinky to her room at night. The affectionate cat slept at the foot of her bed and woke her up at the same time every morning by gently purring in her ear.

Jen poked around the room, looking in all of Slinky's usual hiding spots.

She was about to give up when she saw a scrap of paper under a chair. Realizing it was a piece of the letter Ms. Hartlet had torn to pieces, she picked it up. Only a few scrawled words were visible.

Forgetting about Slinky, Jen charged out of the room and raced after Zeke. He was in the dining room, straightening the chairs for tomorrow's breakfast.

"Look!" She held the paper out to him.

Zeke read out loud: " 'And do whatever it takes to get the job, because . . .' " He turned the paper over. "That's it? What is this? What does it mean?"

Jen explained about Ms. Hartlet's letter and how she had torn it up as though she didn't want anyone to read it.

"Seems really suspicious," Zeke agreed, shaking his head.

"Suspicious how?" Jen asked. She had been thinking the same thing, but it didn't make sense.

A sudden shout startled the twins. It was followed by three loud thumps as though someone was falling down the stairs!

5
Mighty
Suspicious

Jen and Zeke tore into the foyer and looked up the wide front stairs. About halfway down, Mr. Mitchell was slowly easing himself onto his feet.

Aunt Bee appeared in her fluffy green bathrobe, her long hair loose down her back. "What happened?"

Mr. Mitchell stretched his arms as if he was checking for broken bones. "Someone pushed me down the stairs!"

"Surely not," Dr. Bowles said. He and the other guests had rushed out of their rooms and now crowded at both ends of the stairs.

"Then how did I fall?" Mr. Mitchell demanded.

"Perhaps you tripped," Ms. Hartlet suggested.

"Perhaps you pushed me," Mr. Mitchell shot back. "I am not out of shape and clumsy like some people here."

"What makes you think someone pushed you?"

Zeke asked before anyone could open their mouth to protest.

Mr. Mitchell stomped down the stairs. "I felt a hand shove me from behind. Luckily I'm in excellent physical condition and caught myself halfway down. I could have broken my neck!"

"What were you doing upstairs anyway?" Jen asked. She knew she sounded a little rude, but it was pretty strange for him to be on the second floor when his room was on the first.

"I was looking for my stopwatch. It's disappeared."

"And you thought it would be up here?" Mr. Crane asked from the top of the stairs. "Did you think one of us had stolen it?"

"*Somebody* took it," Mr. Mitchell snapped back.

"Now, now," Aunt Bee said soothingly. "I'm sure we'll find it. We do have a mischievous ghost who sometimes hides things. It'll turn up tomorrow. You'll see."

Zeke watched Ms. Hartlet at the top of the stairs, where she stood looking down. Her room was down the hall. Could she have pushed Mr. Mitchell and then ducked around the corner and into her room before anyone saw her?

When they were sure Mr. Mitchell wasn't injured, everyone said good night again. Jen and Zeke heard the locks click after each door shut.

The twins hugged their aunt and headed into the lighthouse tower to their rooms.

"Do you think it was an accident?" Jen asked Zeke.

"I don't know. He said he felt a hand on his back."

"What was he doing upstairs anyway? Did he really lose his stopwatch, or was that just an excuse to be up there?"

"If he did lose it," Zeke said, "why would it be on the second floor?"

~✓~

The next day, during language arts, Jen ran an errand to the office for Mrs. Hay, her teacher. As she stood at the front desk, waiting for the secretary, she noticed that Mr. Crane was talking on the office phone. Jen edged toward him. *It's not that I'm nosy,* she told herself. *Just curious.*

Mr. Crane hunched over the phone. He obviously didn't want anyone to overhear him.

What could possibly be so important and private? Jen wondered.

"I just can't," Mr. Crane said hoarsely into the mouthpiece. He said something else, but it was too soft to hear.

Jen inched closer, her mouth going dry when she

heard Mr. Crane's next few words.

"I can't do it. These people are so . . . It's harder than I thought it would be . . . Didn't go as planned, and neither did the other . . ."

The school secretary startled Jen by asking her what she wanted. By the time she'd finished talking to the secretary, Mr. Crane had left the office.

Jen was dying to tell Zeke what she'd overheard, but it was an hour until lunch, so she went back to class. Finally, the hour passed and Jen found Zeke in the cafeteria, but it was hard to talk over all the noise.

"That sounds suspicious," Zeke said after they had found a quieter corner.

Jen nodded, taking a bite of her peanut butter and banana sandwich.

"Suspicious how?"

"Offf hutting fe offers," Jen said.

Zeke rolled his eyes. "Try swallowing first," he advised.

"Of hurting the others," Jen said again after she'd washed down her bite with some ice-cold milk. "If he can get rid of the other candidates, he'll get the job! Remember, he was the one who pointed out that only one of them could be the principal. He must want it so badly he's willing to do anything to get the others out of the way."

Zeke nodded thoughtfully, chewing a bite of his homemade granola bar.

Before either of them had a chance to say anything more, Stacey appeared with a tray balanced in one hand. She tugged on Jen's arm. "Come on, Jen, you said you'd sit near the windows with me. You won't believe what Josh just told me!"

With a shrug at her brother, Jen stood up and hurried after her friend. She silently sent a message to Zeke. *We'll talk after school.* He must have gotten the message, because when she turned around to look at him, he nodded.

✓

After the school bus dropped them off at the bottom of the hill, the twins trudged up the road to the B&B. "Did you have any brilliant thoughts?" Jen asked.

"About what?"

"About what's going on. There's too much weird stuff happening for it to all be coincidental, don't you think?"

"Maybe."

"What do you mean, maybe?" Jen demanded.

"Maybe we're just overreacting."

"Mr. Mitchell was almost killed falling down the

stairs and Mrs. Adams was practically run over, and you think I'm overreacting?" Jen huffed. "Maybe you're just *under*reacting!"

"There's no such word as underreacting," Zeke said.

Jen glared at him. "Oh, forget it. I'll figure this out on my own."

Inside, they found Detective Wilson sitting at the kitchen table with Aunt Bee. They were laughing over something, and Detective Wilson was finishing off a slice of apple pie à la mode.

Though the detective was retired now, he'd worked on the Mystic police force for forty years, and everyone still called him Detective Wilson. Jen thought he had a crush on Aunt Bee, but Zeke said he just liked her cooking. Either way, they were always glad to see him. He often came for snacks or dinner, and he liked to help Bee with the heavier work around the B&B.

He greeted them now with a smile warm enough to melt any ice cream left on his plate. Of course, there wasn't any ice cream left, Jen noted. When Aunt Bee cooked or baked, there was never anything left on anyone's plate.

Jen plunked down in a chair next to Detective Wilson. "Did Aunt Bee tell you about the accidents?"

The detective raised his eyebrows. "Accidents?"

"It was nothing," Aunt Bee assured him. "That's all they were—*accidents*."

"Maybe," Jen said, "but maybe not." She proceeded to tell the detective about Mrs. Adams's car accident and about Mr. Mitchell claiming to be pushed down the stairs and nearly breaking his neck.

"And don't forget Mr. Crane's missing briefcase," Zeke added.

Detective Wilson listened thoughtfully, then said, "I'm afraid there's nothing the police can do about those incidents unless the victims want to report them. Besides, they do sound like accidents. Even if Mrs. Adams and Mr. Mitchell made reports, it's likely nothing would come of them. And since Mr. Crane found his briefcase . . ." His voice trailed off and he shrugged.

Jen scowled at Zeke, who was giving her a smug smile. Aunt Bee got up and served each of the twins a slice of pie and said, "You'll need to wait to clean the rooms this afternoon. The guests are all resting right now. They have a dinner tonight and a big day of interviews tomorrow. I think the stress is getting to them."

Aunt Bee scooped out a big spoonful of ice cream for Jen. Just as she dropped it onto Jen's piece of pie, a bloodcurdling scream echoed through the B&B.

6
Another Victim

A chilling shiver snaked up Jen's spine. "Who was that?" she whispered.

The scream came again.

Detective Wilson was already on his feet, racing toward the sound. Jen, Zeke, and Aunt Bee followed close behind. They heard a commotion on the second floor and ran up the front stairs. Some of the guests were crowded in the hall outside Ms. Hartlet's room. Ms. Hartlet stood in the middle of the group, her hands over her face as Mrs. Adams tried to comfort her.

"What happened?" Detective Wilson asked.

"A s-s-snake," Ms. Hartlet said through chattering teeth.

Jen and Zeke pushed through the group and

stopped in the doorway. Dr. Bowles was on his hands and knees, looking for the snake under the bed.

"Have you seen it?" Zeke asked.

"Yep," Dr. Bowles grunted. "But it slithered away. Now I can't find it."

"What kind is it?"

"Just the innocent garden variety. Nothing to worry about."

"I'm not worried," Zeke said. "I'll help you look for it."

Jen joined the search. She didn't love snakes, but at least she knew this one wasn't poisonous. As she crawled around on the floor she thought, *That snake didn't get in here on its own. Something is definitely going on.*

She found the snake curled around the base of the wastebasket, right near the heater. After swallowing .a little screech, she called to Zeke and Dr. Bowles. She tried to keep her voice steady. "I found it."

Dr. Bowles scooped up the snake with one hand. The other guests gave him a lot of space as he exited Ms. Hartlet's room.

"Just a cute little garter snake," Dr. Bowles said with a hearty chuckle as he made his way down the stairs to bring the snake outdoors. Halfway down, he passed Mr. Mitchell and thrust the snake toward him. "Would you like to take it outside?"

Mr. Mitchell lurched back so far that Jen was sure he was about to fall backward over the banister. When he righted himself, she had to bite her lip to keep from laughing out loud.

"No, thanks," Mr. Mitchell said, still leaning away from the snake. "Looks like you have everything under control."

Dr. Bowles grinned. "If you're sure." He proceeded down the rest of the stairs and out the front door, chuckling the whole way.

Mr. Mitchell stared after him with his eyes narrowed and his lips pulled into a slash of annoyance.

If looks could kill, Zeke couldn't help thinking.

Ms. Hartlet had to be reassured several times that there weren't any more snakes in her room before she would go back in. Mr. Crane, whose room was across the hall, looked a little pale—especially when Mrs. Adams said, "I certainly hope there aren't snakes in any other rooms!"

Aunt Bee cleared her throat. "I can't imagine how the snake got in here, but there must be a logical explanation. This has never happened before."

Jen pulled on Zeke's arm, leading him downstairs and into the parlor. "See?" she hissed. "Something strange *is* going on. Someone tried to run Mrs. Adams off the cliff at Dead Man's Curve, someone stole Mr.

Crane's briefcase with all his important papers inside, someone shoved Mr. Mitchell down the stairs so that he almost broke his neck, and Ms. Hartlet was scared stiff."

Zeke nodded. "Maybe it isn't all so coincidental after all."

"Not only that," Jen said, "but the person responsible has to be someone staying here."

"Why?"

"Aunt Bee would have noticed a stranger coming in to drop off the snake. And last night she had locked up before Mr. Mitchell was pushed down the stairs. Obviously, someone wants the job so bad they're trying to scare away the competition."

"You're right," Zeke agreed.

"So we have to figure out who's causing all these accidents before someone gets hurt."

"But I'm sure Detective Wilson is going to do that."

Jen flopped on the couch with a little groan. "Who knows more about the guests? Detective Wilson or us? We'll figure out who it is and then tell him."

"Just a little sleuthing, right?"

"Exactly," Jen agreed. "So where do we start?"

"We'll have to examine the scene of each accident. Let's start with the first one and go from there."

Jen cringed. "That means we have to go to Dead Man's Curve!"

Dead Man's Curve

"Right. Dead Man's Curve," Zeke repeated. That dangerous S-turn in the road always gave him the willies. Calling it Dead Man's Curve, as the locals did, didn't help any. There were tons of accidents there each year. The city had recently repaved the road and put up a new guardrail, hoping to avoid more accidents. Obviously it hadn't worked—Mrs. Adams had had the first accident since they had improved the road.

"We'll go tomorrow," Jen said. "The teachers are having that in-service conference all day, so we'll be free to investigate."

"Did I hear you say you'll be free tomorrow?" Aunt Bee asked, stepping into the parlor. "Have you forgotten about painting the molding around the windows in the dining room and parlor?"

"But that could take all day," Jen wailed.

Aunt Bee winked at her. "You can start now if you'd like." With a grin, she left.

Jen and Zeke looked at each other. They didn't relish the idea of starting now, but what about their trip to Dead Man's Curve?

"We have to go look for clues right now," Jen said, looking at her watch.

"But it'll be getting dark soon."

"Not for at least another hour. Come on." She stood up.

Aunt Bee stepped back into the parlor. "I need you to help me in the kitchen for a while, Jen. No offense, Zeke, but your sister is better at kneading dough. All those years of playing softball have given her the strong hands needed for dough. Get it? Kneaded? Needed?" She grinned so wide her silver fillings shone.

Still grinning, she left again and Jen looked at her twin. "You'll just have to go to Dead Man's Curve alone."

Zeke swallowed hard. "Alone?" he repeated.

Jen nodded. "Can you think of another idea? I have to stay here and help Aunt Bee now, and tomorrow we have tons of work. This will be our—I mean *your* only chance."

"I guess so," Zeke said reluctantly, trying to think of another plan.

"You do want to solve this mystery, don't you?" Jen asked.

"Of course, but—"

"Then get going. Ride your bike and just be careful when you get to Dead Man's Curve."

"Gee, thanks for the advice," Zeke said, rolling his eyes.

As they left the parlor, Zeke looked around. He could have sworn he'd heard the creak of a footstep out here a second ago, but no one was in sight. He shrugged it off, figuring it must have been Aunt Bee.

Jen walked with him back to where they kept their bikes. She watched as her twin covered his wavy brown hair with a bright red helmet.

"Good luck," she said.

"Thanks." With that, Zeke pedaled off down the hill. He rode on the right side of the road—"with traffic," although there were very few cars.

Going downhill was easy. Zeke let the bike coast along. He tried not to think about Dead Man's Curve. But the more he tried not to think about it, the more he *did* think about it. *Dead Man's Curve. Dead Man's Curve. Dead Man's Curve. Argh!*

When the sloping road from the lighthouse leveled out, Zeke had to start pedaling. The sun was low in the sky behind the pine trees to his right as he

headed south. At least the dreaded curve in the road wasn't too far away. He figured he should be able to get there and back to the B&B within thirty to forty-five minutes tops.

He pedaled faster. Not that he was eager to get there, he just wanted to get this over with. As he neared the curve, his fingers gripped the handlebars tighter and tighter.

The road eased around a gentle turn, and then it suddenly bent into Dead Man's Curve. On the other side of the road was some grass, then a railing, and then nothing. The cliff dropped off to the smashing waves and sharp rocks below. This side of the road was hilly and shadowed by pine trees. Zeke rode on the dirt shoulder, staying as far from the pavement as possible. A few cars passed him, but they all moved at a safe speed, wisely heeding the yellow arrows and the signs that read SLOW DOWN, DANGEROUS CURVE AHEAD.

At last he reached the spot where, from her description, Mrs. Adams had been run off the road. He got off his bike and then very carefully walked with it across both lanes. He parked it in a ditch, avoiding the sheer drop right beside him, on the other side of the guardrail. He tried not to look over the edge. *It's not that I'm afraid of heights*, he told himself, *it's just that*—his mind went blank. *Okay, so I don't like heights*, he thought. He hated to admit it, even to himself.

Trying to ignore the cliff and the crashing waves below, Zeke began to look around for clues. Strong gusts of wind battered him, rustling the trees and blowing loose soil into his eyes. Squinting, he examined the road from where he stood. He didn't see any skid marks, which was a little strange. Maybe Mrs. Adams had exaggerated about how bad her accident had been.

Next he looked for pieces of plastic from the broken taillight, but with the wind blowing every which way, he wasn't surprised not to see any on the road. He got down on his hands and knees and checked in the grass along the side of the road by the guardrail. All he found was a 1950 nickel, a soda can, two old shoes that didn't match, and a marble. No bits of broken taillight.

Finally Zeke gave up. Sitting back on his heels, he looked around, wondering if he'd missed a spot. The sun hadn't set yet, but it was hidden behind the pine trees on the other side of the road. Zeke shivered and zipped up his jacket. It was getting darker and windier by the second. He hated to leave without finding anything important, but Aunt Bee didn't like either of the twins to be out after dark on their bikes.

He walked back to his bike, kicking the grass along

the way. He hoped to see the glint of broken pieces of red or white plastic. Something caught his eye, but when he bent closer to look, it was only a rusty scrap of metal. The sun was setting behind the pine trees and it was getting hard to see much of anything.

Suddenly, the roar of a car engine thundered behind him. He felt as if he were caught in a slow-motion movie as he turned around. Two giant glowing headlights had crossed the center line and were headed right for him! Without thinking, he jumped out of the way. He landed in the grass, twisting his right ankle. Then he tumbled to the ground. A sharp pain jabbed up his leg.

At the last possible second, the car swerved away from him and whizzed around the curve on screeching tires. The next second it was out of sight.

Zeke clutched his sore ankle. *What am I going to do now?* he wondered. No way could he ride his bike home, but Aunt Bee would kill him if she knew what had happened. He had to get home, no matter how much his ankle hurt.

He tried to calm down, but his heart wouldn't stop hammering behind his ribs.

Only one thought kept racing through his mind. Someone had tried to kill him. What if that someone came back to finish the job?

8
No Clue

Jen looked at her watch again, then glanced out the large kitchen window. It was nearly dark and Zeke had been gone for over an hour. He should have been back by now.

"What on earth are you doing?" Aunt Bee asked, peering over her niece's shoulder.

Jen looked down at the dough she was supposed to be kneading. But instead of pushing it this way and that, punching it, and throwing it down on the table as she was supposed to do, she had torn off little pieces and rolled them into balls the size of marbles.

"Sorry," Jen said, quickly trying to mush the dough back together again. "I guess I was distracted."

"By what?"

"Zeke should have been back by now," Jen blurted out.

"Back from where?"

"He—he went to Dead Man's Curve."

"At this time of day?" Aunt Bee asked, starting to untie her bee-dotted apron. "It's nearly dark. That's a dangerous piece of road, especially at twilight."

"I know," Jen said, rubbing dough off her fingers. "I'm worried about him."

Aunt Bee grabbed a large set of keys that hung from a peg. "Come on. We'd better go find him."

Jen ran after her aunt, and they buckled up in Aunt Bee's station wagon. They zoomed down the hill and along the coast road to Dead Man's Curve.

Glancing to the side, Jen saw that her aunt's lips were pressed into a thin line.

"I'm sorry," she said, her voice barely loud enough to be heard over the sound of the engine.

"You two should know better than to go to such a dangerous piece of road at sunset. Dusk is the worst possible time for drivers. It's hard to see."

Jen gripped the edges of her seat. She tried to focus in on Zeke. But as hard as she concentrated, all she felt was a sudden jab of pain in her ankle, which couldn't possibly mean anything. Or could it?

"There he is!" Jen shouted as they neared Dead Man's Curve.

Aunt Bee put on the brakes and carefully pulled to the side of the road, leaving the car lights on to warn any other traffic. The headlights shone on Zeke. He was pushing his bike and limping along beside it.

Jen and Aunt Bee hurried to meet him.

"Zeke, what happened?" Aunt Bee asked.

"It's your ankle, isn't it?" Jen said, suddenly realizing why she'd gotten the pain in her ankle when she was trying to connect with her brother.

Zeke nodded. "I twisted my ankle. I don't think it's broken, though."

"Let's get you home," Aunt Bee said. She helped her nephew to the car, while Jen rolled his bike over to it. They put the bike in the back and Zeke sprawled across the rear seat.

"I thought you guys would never come," he said once they were back on the road.

"We came as soon as Jennifer told me where you were and that you were late," Aunt Bee said.

Jen looked over the back of the seat at Zeke. They knew Aunt Bee was upset whenever she used their full names.

Slowly and carefully, Aunt Bee eased the large car around the tricky corners of Dead Man's Curve.

Jen fidgeted in the front seat. She had a feeling something major had happened to Zeke. There were so many questions she wanted to ask her brother, but not in front of their aunt. Aunt Bee would only worry and tell them not to get involved.

When they reached Quick Stop Mart, Aunt Bee pulled into the parking lot and handed Jen some money. "We're low on ice cream."

Jen hopped out and dashed into the store. She grabbed a gallon of vanilla and took it to the check-out counter.

"Hey, Jen," the clerk said.

Jen smiled at her best friend's older brother. "Hi, Brian. Do you like your new job?"

"It's okay," he said, ringing up her purchase. "Sometimes it's hard to get here on time, but I like payday, that's for sure!"

Jen laughed and shook her head when he offered her a red-white-and-blue-striped plastic bag for the ice cream. "I'm trying to save the environment. See you later, Brian."

She hopped in the car and Aunt Bee pulled out, heading toward home.

Jen held her breath as they once again negotiated the hairpin turns. Only this time she could look down the cliff on her right to the inky blackness of the ocean roaring beneath them. It seemed like they all breathed easier once they were past Dead Man's Curve.

When they reached the B&B, Aunt Bee turned to them before getting out of the car. "I don't know what you two are getting into," she said sternly. "But I want you both to be more careful. Do you understand?"

Zeke and Jen nodded solemnly.

Aunt Bee helped Zeke into the parlor where he could put ice on his ankle and eat dinner.

It wasn't until after they'd eaten that Jen had a chance to talk to Zeke alone. "So what happened out there?" she asked.

"A car almost hit me. I hurt my ankle jumping out of the way."

"What?! Was it an accident, or did someone try to hit you?" she asked.

Zeke shook his head. "The car came pretty close. Too close. It either meant to hit me, or scare me over the edge of the cliff."

"You must have been scared stiff."

"Nah," Zeke said. "It was nothing."

Jen narrowed her eyes at her twin.

Zeke grinned. "Okay, maybe a little scared," he admitted with a laugh. "That's the one bad thing about being a twin," he added. "I can't get anything past you!"

Jen laughed, too, realizing how relieved she was that her brother was back at home, safe and sound. "So what does it mean? Why did someone try to ki— hurt you?" She just couldn't say *kill*.

"I have no idea," Zeke admitted. "Maybe we know

something we're not supposed to know and one of the guests is getting nervous."

They thought for a moment in silence. Then Jen said, "What did the car that tried to hit you look like?"

"I don't know," Zeke admitted. "It all happened so fast. At the last moment I saw the car speed off around the corner, but it was too fast and too dark to see it."

"That means it could have been anyone."

"Oh, great. Someone is trying to get rid of us because we know too much, and we don't have a clue!"

⌇

The next morning, Zeke's ankle was feeling better.

"Good," Jen said. "You can help paint the window trim."

"I don't know if it feels good enough for all that work."

Jen glared at her twin. "It's going to feel a lot worse if you *don't* help me," she threatened.

"Ooooh, my little sister is going to hurt me."

Jen took a swipe at him, but even with a slightly sprained ankle, he was too quick. He hopped away, laughing.

Aunt Bee set them up in the dining room, assigning Zeke work he could do mostly sitting down and giving Jen the upper areas.

They finally finished around noon.

"Can you put everything away?" Zeke asked. "My ankle is kind of throbbing again."

Jen eyed her brother, trying to figure out if he was just trying to get out of more work. He did look a little pale. "Don't worry. I'll do it."

She piled all the paint cans and brushes into a box and headed out the back door where she passed Mr. Mitchell coming in. He looked startled to see her.

Jen smiled. "Hi. Can I help you with something?" She hadn't meant to sound nosy, but the way Mr. Mitchell's face turned red, she got the feeling she had asked the wrong question.

"No, thanks," he mumbled and hurried away.

Jen shrugged, wondering what he was up to, and headed toward the storage shed. Plodding along, head bent, at first she didn't notice anyone in the parking lot. Then she saw Mrs. Adams rummaging around in the trunk of her car. Putting down the box with a sigh of relief, Jen walked over.

"Do you need help with something?"

Mrs. Adams shrieked and slammed the trunk shut. "Oh! You scared the daylights out of me!"

9

Coughing
to Death

"Sorry," Jen said. "I didn't mean to sneak up on you. I just thought you might need help getting something out of your trunk."

Mrs. Adams laughed breathlessly, a fluttering hand still pressed against her throat. "Oh, no. I was just trying to rearrange it a bit. I've bought so many souvenirs at the local shops, I wanted to be sure they will all fit in when I leave. Of course," she lowered her voice, "I have every reason to believe I'll be coming back very soon."

"Are you going to get the job?" Jen asked.

Throwing up her hands, Mrs. Adams said, "I can't be positive, but I do have a good feeling about it."

Jen smiled and nodded toward the box of paints. "I guess I'd better get back to work. See you later."

With a cheery wave, Mrs. Adams headed into the B&B.

Jen stored the paint in the shed and found Zeke in the kitchen washing his hands.

"Everyone's back from the interviews," she said. "I just saw Mrs. Adams in the parking lot. She bought a bunch of stuff in town and she's trying to figure out how to fit it all into her trunk. All I saw in there was a toolbox, so she should have plenty of room."

"A toolbox?" Zeke asked, wiping his hands dry. "Why does she have a toolbox in her trunk?"

"What's so strange about that?" Jen asked, turning to wash her hands. "Aunt Bee keeps hers under the sink."

Zeke shrugged. "You're right. I guess all you females are strange."

He laughed. But then, in a sudden burst of pain, he winced. "Oooh, my aching ankle. I don't think I can help you clean the rooms, Jen."

"You're faking it," she protested.

"No, it really, really hurts." He limped over to a chair.

"I'll get you for this! Just wait!" With her brother's laughter ringing in her ears, she gathered up the cleaning supplies and left the kitchen.

Though the guests had just finished up a day of intensive interviews, most were not in their rooms. Instead of following the strict order Zeke had set for when they cleaned, Jen decided to mix up the rooms just for fun.

Dr. Bowles was out for a walk so she went to his room first. As she cleaned, quietly whistling to herself, she sensed that something wasn't right. But she couldn't quite put her finger on what it was. With a shrug, she finished up and moved on to the next room.

It wasn't until Jen was sweeping Mrs. Adams's floor that she realized what had seemed strange about Dr. Bowles's room. His carved box was missing!

Mrs. Adams showed up just as Jen was locking the woman's door. "My goodness, but you do work hard," Mrs. Adams said.

"Just part of living at a B&B," Jen responded. "But I really don't mind." Jen excused herself then and moved down the hall. She lugged her pail through the foyer, where she met Mr. Mitchell heading out for a jog.

"I'm going to clean your room," she called after him. "Is that okay?"

"Go ahead," he said over his shoulder. "Doesn't need much cleaning, though." He closed the front door behind him.

Jen grinned when she peeked into his room. She was the only person she knew who would agree with him. But even for her the mess was a bit extreme.

Leaving the door open, she began sweeping wherever she could set the broom down on the floor. That took about two minutes since not a lot of floor showed between the shoes, magazines, and clothes.

Someone coughed behind her while she was scrubbing the bathroom sink.

Startled, Jen whirled around to come eye to eye with a slightly hunched-over Mrs. Adams. "Oh, it's you," she said with relief, only now realizing how on edge she felt. She was sure she'd be a lot more relaxed when they'd solved this mystery.

Mrs. Adams coughed again, holding a large handkerchief to her mouth. Her face turned brighter than her hair as the coughing continued.

Beginning to feel alarmed, Jen asked, "Are you okay?"

The woman shook her head.

Daggers of alarm shot through Jen. "Did—did someone poison you?"

"No," Mrs. Adams croaked out. "Water."

"You need some water?"

Mrs. Adams nodded vigorously.

Still feeling a bit alarmed, Jen looked at the glass on Mr. Mitchell's sink. It had toothpaste drippings on the side. Ick.

"I'll be right back," Jen said. She ran out of the

room and through the dining room to the kitchen. Jen grabbed a clean glass and filled it with cold water from the tap. She ran back to Mr. Mitchell's room. The room was empty, but she heard coughing coming from down the hall. It wasn't hard to follow the hacking sound to Mrs. Adams's room.

Jen handed her the water.

Her bright red face faded as Mrs. Adams drank nearly half the glass, then gasped for breath. "Oh, thank you, dear." She coughed again and finished the water. "My goodness. Something started to tickle my throat and it simply wouldn't stop. I thought I'd expire!"

"Like the date on a milk carton?" Jen asked, puzzled.

Mrs. Adams laughed. "In a way. To expire in this case means to simply pass away. To die."

Jen shivered. "Well, I'm glad you didn't—uh—expire," she said. Then she laughed as Slinky scooted out from under the bed with Mrs. Adams's handkerchief between her teeth.

"Oh, dear," Mrs. Adams said, looking startled.

Jen picked up the long-haired cat. "Naughty kitty," she said, hugging Slinky. "Sorry about that. Slinky is more curious than most cats."

Mrs. Adams pulled her handkerchief away, then Jen tossed the cat out the door. "If you keep your door closed, she won't bother you."

"I'll remember that. Thank you so much for the water, dear. My glass is full of flowers. You saved my life."

Jen grinned. "Just one of my jobs around here." With that, she hurried back to Mr. Mitchell's room and quickly finished cleaning. It was a nice day, and she'd rather be outside tossing a softball with Stacey.

She worked her way upstairs, dusting the banister as she went. Remembering their plan to inspect the scene of every accident, Jen bent over and examined the carpet at the top of the stairs. She peered at it closely, but there was no bump or tear that could have tripped Mr. Mitchell. Someone *must* have pushed him down the stairs. Either that or he faked it. She sighed. They weren't any closer to solving the mystery.

Ms. Hartlet had left a note on her door not to disturb her. Jen stood outside her door a moment and wondered how someone could have put a snake in the room. The crack under the door didn't seem big enough. The only way was for someone to drop the snake through the ventilation window above the door. The house was so old that it was built with small windows above every door so that even when the doors were closed, a breeze could flow through the rooms. But knowing *how* it was done didn't help solve *who'd* done it.

When she knocked on Mr. Crane's door, no one answered. Jen popped her head in, happy to see that his room looked as tidy as ever—not a scrap of paper out of place. Cleaning it took no time at all.

Lugging the broom, dustpan, and bucket with cleaning solvents out of the room, she locked the door behind her.

"Where is it!" a man's voice bellowed downstairs. "Who took it?"

10
Eavesdropping

Jen dropped everything and nearly flew down the stairs. She knew only one person with a voice that deep.

Sure enough, Dr. Bowles stood in his doorway, his round face purple with anger. "Someone stole my box!"

By now, everyone had gathered except Mr. Mitchell, who was still out running. Even Zeke had hobbled into the foyer to see what was going on.

"Someone stole my box right out of my room. I must find it!"

"Why would someone want to steal it?" Zeke asked Jen quietly.

"Maybe it's an antique and worth a lot of money."

"Or maybe there's something valuable inside it, and that's why he keeps it locked."

Aunt Bee patted the large man's arm. "I'm sure we'll find it," she said soothingly. "We can all look for it right now. What does it look like?"

Dr. Bowles described the size, color, and the dragon design on the box, including the initials carved above the lock.

Mr. Crane said he'd look upstairs, but Zeke heard him go into his room and lock the door. Everyone else spread out to hunt for the missing box.

Jen followed Ms. Hartlet and Mrs. Adams into the dining room. Mrs. Adams said quietly, "I don't know what all the fuss is about. The man is so absent-minded, he probably left it somewhere himself."

As the two women scouted around the dining room, Jen looked through the kitchen, not expecting to find the box. She did find a fresh batch of peanut butter cookies, though, and stopped to quickly refuel her growling stomach.

Meanwhile, Zeke limped into the parlor. Even though he knew Jen thought he was exaggerating about his ankle, it really did throb. Looking for a stolen box didn't sound like much fun.

He sat on the floor to rest for a bit. Woofer lunged over to him, put his paws on Zeke's shoulders, and pushed him over.

"Enough, Woofer," Zeke said with a laugh as the dog licked his ear. But Woofer was too strong to easily push away and too stubborn to stop.

The hot, sloppy tongue tickled, and Zeke rolled on the floor laughing. "Stop it, Woofer!"

Zeke was twisting around, trying to keep his sore ankle out of Woofer's clumsy way, when he spotted something brown and square under the easy chair in the corner. He pushed the dog away and crawled to the chair. He reached under it and pulled out Dr. Bowles's box.

Jen walked into the parlor at that moment. "You found it!" she exclaimed when she saw what he held in his hands. "Where was it?"

"Right under this chair."

"I wonder who hid it there."

"Mr. Crane maybe?" Zeke suggested.

"But why would he do that? It doesn't make any sense."

"Nothing about this case makes sense."

Jen lifted her eyebrows. "Case? That's a box, not a case."

"I was talking about the case we're trying to solve. You know, the mystery of who's causing all these accidents?"

"Oh, right, the case," Jen said, rolling her eyes. "I think you've been reading too many mysteries," she added with a grin. Then she called, "We found it!"

Footsteps thumped toward the room. Dr. Bowles

burst into the parlor. He snatched the box out of Zeke's hands, closely examining the lock.

"Where was it?" the man asked.

Zeke pointed. "Under that chair."

For a second, Dr. Bowles looked surprised. "Oh." With that, he turned and abruptly left the room. A moment later they heard him call, "Thanks."

The twins sat on the sofa with Woofer asleep at their feet. Now that the box had been found, the B&B was quiet again. Too quiet. Jen could feel herself get sleepy. Just as she started to doze off, she heard a voice coming from the foyer. She and Zeke looked at each other.

Jen put a finger to her lips.

Zeke silently mouthed the words, "Mr. Crane."

Nodding, Jen stood and tiptoed toward the parlor door to hear better.

"It's all falling apart," Mr. Crane said. He was obviously talking on the phone that was kept at the front desk. None of the rooms had private phones.

His voice faded out, then she heard, "People suspicious . . ."

Jen took a step closer to hear better. Behind her, Zeke hopped closer, too. He landed on a squeaky board. It screeched like an angry cat. The twins froze. The voice in the foyer stopped abruptly.

A moment later, Mr. Crane said, "I have to go. I love you, too, dear."

The twins heard the phone click down in its cradle. They hustled back to the couch. Sure enough, a second later, Mr. Crane stuck his head into the room. "Do you two always eavesdrop on private calls?" Without waiting for an answer he snapped, "For your information, I was talking to my wife."

Jen and Zeke slouched lower in their seats after Mr. Crane left. "He must think we're a couple of snoops," Jen said.

"I don't think this is what Aunt Bee meant when she said we should make a good impression. If Mr. Crane is our next principal, we're in big trouble!"

"You said it."

"But do you think he really was talking to his wife?" Zeke asked.

"He said *I love you* to someone."

"Maybe that was just a cover-up. Everything else sounded pretty suspicious."

As they sat there thinking, Mr. Mitchell came back from his run. He popped his head into the parlor and said, "Could I get something cold to drink? I just ran ten miles."

Jen jumped up. "Sure. I'll get something from the kitchen."

Mr. Mitchell followed her. She filled a large glass with water. He drank it down in less than thirty seconds. "Whew, that tasted great," he said, wiping sweat off his brow. "Nothing like water to quench your thirst."

Jen opened her mouth to respond when a crash and crackle of breaking glass filled the air!

11

Leave Now or Else!

Jen's heart raced faster than her legs could carry her down the hall. Mr. Mitchell stayed close at her heels. By the time she'd found the source of the commotion, she was out of breath. The guests were packed just inside the door to Mrs. Adams's room. Jen pushed between bodies to the front of the group so that she could see what was going on. Zeke was already there.

"What happened?" she gasped.

Zeke pointed.

A dumbbell lay on the floor. A piece of paper was taped to it. Shards of glass shimmered all around. With a sinking heart, Jen realized someone had thrown the dumbbell through Mrs. Adams's window.

"It's Mr. Mitchell's," Jen commented to her brother.

He nodded. "Obviously someone threw it."

"But who?"

Mrs. Adams sat on the edge of her bed, her face in her hands. "This is terrible," she wailed. "Just terrible."

Aunt Bee tried to calm her. "Don't worry. I'm sure we'll get to the bottom of this." Then Aunt Bee stepped gingerly over to the weight and plucked the piece of paper off it. She read out loud, "'Leave now or else!'"

Dr. Bowles stepped forward. "Let me see that." Aunt Bee handed him the note and he examined it closely before passing it on to Ms. Hartlet, who handed it to Mr. Crane. Everyone got a good look at the letter except the twins. When the note circled around to Aunt Bee again, she stuffed it into the pocket of her skirt without showing it to Jen and Zeke.

Mrs. Adams couldn't stop crying. "Who would do such a thing?"

Everyone glanced at one another.

"Whose dumbbell is it?" Ms. Hartlet asked.

Mr. Mitchell stepped forward. "It's mine, but I didn't throw it through the window."

"Someone did," Dr. Bowles said. "And if it's your dumbbell . . ." He let his voice trail off.

Mr. Mitchell clenched his fists. "I didn't do it. I was in the kitchen when I heard the window breaking." He turned to Jen. "Isn't that right?"

Jen nodded. "He couldn't have done it."

"When did you notice you were missing a dumb-bell?" Mrs. Adams used her large white handkerchief to dab at her eyes. "You must have realized it was gone."

Zeke leaned closer to Jen and whispered, "How could he notice anything in his mess of a room?"

Jen jabbed her brother in the side. "Very funny," she whispered back. But she had to admit Zeke did have a point. How many times had she "lost" something in her room when it was just hidden under a sweatshirt or a pile of books?

"I've had enough of this," Mr. Mitchell said, throwing up his hands. "I'm leaving! I'm sure I would have gotten the position, but no job is worth getting hurt over! This has become ridiculous." With that, he stormed out of the room.

For a moment, no one said anything. Then Aunt Bee cleared her throat. "I'm so sorry this has happened. I don't know how to explain it. Perhaps we should call the police?"

"That seems a bit extreme," Mrs. Adams said, taking a steadying breath. "None of this is going to scare me off, though I wouldn't blame any of you for leaving. Mr. Mitchell has the right idea. I'm just too stubborn to give up."

"Could it really be one of us doing all this?" Ms.

Hartlet asked, nervously sweeping loose strands of hair back into her bun.

Mr. Crane snorted. "Who else could it be? Now, if you'll excuse me, I have to prepare for the last round of interviews." He left without another word.

Dr. Bowles and Ms. Hartlet excused themselves, too.

Aunt Bee patted Mrs. Adams on the shoulder. "Are you sure you'll be all right?" When she nodded, Aunt Bee said, "The twins will clean up the glass, and I'll get the window boarded up right away."

While Jen fetched the vacuum and a box to put the glass in, Zeke gingerly moved the weight out of the way. It was really heavy, and with his sore ankle, it was hard to lug it clear of the broken glass. Mrs. Adams didn't offer to help. She just sniffled from her bed.

After Jen and Zeke had put all the visible pieces of glass into the box, Jen ran a vacuum over the floor to suck up the tiny slivers.

The twins left the room, carrying the dumbbell and the box of glass with them.

"Thank you, dears," Mrs. Adams called after them.

"No problem," Zeke called back before he shut the door.

"We'd better clean up the glass outside the window," Jen suggested.

Zeke shrugged. "I guess we can, but most of the

glass should have fallen inside from the force of the weight smashing through the window."

They left the heavy dumbbell on the check-in desk and exited the B&B. Walking around the perimeter of the house, they stopped outside Mrs. Adams's first-floor window.

"I told you," Jen said triumphantly, pointing to the pieces of glass glimmering in the afternoon sunlight. "Glass can fall the other way, too."

"You just think you're so smart," Zeke teased his twin.

Jen grinned. "I don't *think* it, I *know* it!"

Laughing, they picked up the rest of the glass and added it to the pile already in the box.

"I'll take it to the bins," Jen offered when they were done. She could see that Zeke's ankle was bothering him again.

Zeke flashed her a grateful smile. "Thanks."

Jen watched him limp away, then she carried the box to the recycling bins they kept on the side of the house next to the garbage.

Just as she was rounding the corner of the house, she saw Mr. Mitchell stuff his last bag into his trunk, slam it closed, get in the car, and zoom off without looking back. Jen grinned. What a wimp. He pretended to be so tough, but look at who was the first one to take off. At least she and Zeke hadn't had to help him with all his luggage!

She dumped the glass in the glass bin and put the box in the paper bin. Slinky appeared out of nowhere and pounced at her foot. Jen laughed. Then the cat batted at a piece of red plastic before diving between two of the bins. A second later, the cat tugged on a red-white-and-blue bag that had somehow gotten stuck between the bins. Jen was just about to reach down and help Slinky when she heard a car pull into the driveway behind her. She waved as Detective Wilson pulled up in his silver SUV.

"Did Aunt Bee call you?" Jen asked after he parked.

He nodded as they walked into the B&B together. "Asked me to board up a window. Someone threw a dumbbell through it?"

"Yep." She told him the story. "Look." She pointed to the check-in desk. "Mr. Mitchell didn't take his weight with him. He must have been so upset he forgot."

"Hmmm," Detective Wilson murmured. "I wonder if we can get fingerprints off it."

"Fingerprints? You mean, like, *real* fingerprints?"

Detective Wilson laughed. "Isn't that the only kind? Now, did you or anyone else touch it?" Clasping his hands behind his back, he looked closely at the plastic-covered weight.

Jen thought a moment. "Zeke picked it up, and I put it over here, but I didn't see anyone else touch it."

Detective Wilson nodded. "Great. Then if we find anyone's prints besides yours, Zeke's, and Mr. Mitchell's, we'll have the guilty person!"

12

Dusting for Prints

"Wow, it's that easy?" Jen asked.

"Not necessarily," Detective Wilson admitted. "But it's a good place to start."

"A good place to start what?" Zeke asked, hopping into the foyer.

Detective Wilson's bushy eyebrows pulled together. "What happened to you?"

Zeke waved his hand like it was nothing. Then he told the retired detective about his bike ride to Dead Man's Curve.

"I don't like the sound of this," Detective Wilson said thoughtfully when Zeke was through with his story. "The sooner we find out who's doing this, the better. Let's get started on the fingerprinting."

Jen looked at the dumbbell closely. "So how do we see the fingerprints?"

"You can't see them until you brush special powder over the object. Then, all of a sudden, fingerprints appear all over it," Detective Wilson explained.

"Let's get going," Zeke said. "What kind of dust do we use?"

"That could be a problem," the detective said, scratching his chin. "The police use dust made especially for fingerprinting. It's very fine, and it comes in different colors. It's also made of different chemicals depending on what they want to lift the fingerprint from."

"You mean they use different powders for glass and paper?" Zeke asked.

"Exactly."

"Powder like baby powder?"

"Oh, no," Detective Wilson said. "That isn't fine enough. But we can make our own fingerprinting powder out of charcoal."

"How?" Zeke asked.

"We'd have to grind the charcoal into a very fine dust, right?" Jen asked.

"Right."

"We could use a mortar and pestle," she added. "Aunt Bee keeps one in the kitchen for crushing nuts."

Detective Wilson smiled. "Perfect. We'll also

need a very fluffy brush, some clear tape, and a sheet of white paper."

"I'll get everything," Jen offered.

"We'll meet you in the kitchen."

Jen trotted off and Detective Wilson pulled a large bandanna out of his pocket. Zeke watched as he used the square of red cloth to pick up the dumbbell. "This way we won't contaminate it with my prints," he explained as they moved to the kitchen and waited for Jen to return.

She met them at the kitchen table with her arms full. She'd found a chunk of charcoal from a bonfire outside. Then Jen triumphantly held up the large fluffy brush she had found. "A blush brush!"

"Good thinking," Zeke said. "Where did you find it?"

Jen gulped. "Uh, with Aunt Bee's makeup and stuff. She doesn't ever use it. And it's for a very good cause." *A little charcoal won't hurt the brush, right?* she thought.

She brought the mortar and pestle over to the table, and Zeke proceeded to grind a hunk of the charcoal into a fine dust. Jen leaned over to inspect his work.

"Looking good," she said. Then a sudden tickle in her nose erupted into a sneeze. All the black powder in the mortar exploded into the air. Jen sneezed again.

"Good going," Zeke cried. His hands and arms were covered with charcoal dust.

Detective Wilson laughed. "The dust must be making you sneeze. You'd better stand back a little."

With an extra-heavy sigh just for his sister's benefit, Zeke started to grind another piece of charcoal. This time he finished without anyone sneezing.

Very carefully, using the blush brush, the detective brushed some of the fine powder across the dumbbell.

Zeke held his breath. In a couple of seconds they'd know who was behind all the dangerous accidents.

Sure enough, as Detective Wilson ran the soft brush over the plastic, the fine black powder clung to smudgy fingerprints. Zeke moved in closer, peering at the prints. He knew what fingerprints should look like, and these marks only looked like black blobs.

"Aha!" Detective Wilson exclaimed.

Jen and Zeke leaned in even closer. "What?" they said at the same time.

Detective Wilson explained that most of the blobs were no good, just as Zeke had thought. But on the side of the dumbbell, there was one perfect fingerprint.

He tore off a piece of clear tape and pressed it against the dumbbell, perfectly covering the black print. Then he lifted the tape in one smooth motion. "If you don't do this carefully," Detective Wilson explained, "you'll create lines through the fingerprint that will get in the way when you're trying to identify it." He gently affixed the tape to a piece of white paper.

Once he had finished lifting the first print, he brushed the other side of the weight. They found four more perfect prints. But on closer inspection, they all agreed that two of them looked exactly like the one they'd already lifted. The other two were different, so they lifted them and taped them next to the first one on the white paper. The second two prints were much smaller than the first.

Detective Wilson thoughtfully tapped the blush brush on the side of the table. "I'm afraid these prints aren't going to help us very much after all."

"Why not?" Jen asked.

"The larger prints are all the same, right?"

Jen and Zeke nodded.

"I think we'll find those prints belong to Mr. Mitchell. And these two smaller prints belong to you two. We can fingerprint you to be sure, but I'll bet your aunt Bee's next apple pie on it."

Zeke felt any remaining hope drain out of him.

Jen rushed out of the kitchen and returned holding a glass in a napkin. "Mr. Mitchell used this to drink water. Let's compare prints on this to the prints we already have."

They fingerprinted it and, sure enough, the prints matched exactly. Then the twins fingerprinted each other and found that the smaller prints on the dumbbell were theirs.

Zeke sighed. "Whoever threw this through the window must have worn gloves—"

"Ms. Hartlet had gloves in her room," Jen interrupted excitedly. "And she was acting so nervous before in Mrs. Adams's room!"

"That doesn't mean she's guilty," Detective Wilson reminded the twins. "Somebody could have used a paper towel or cloth. Anything to keep fingerprints off the weight. I'm afraid this was a waste of time."

"Not really," Jen said with a grin. "Now I know how to take fingerprints so I'll know if Zeke borrows any of my CDs without asking."

Zeke smiled. "I'll trick you." He held up his hands and wiggled his fingers. "Gloves!"

Jen laughed. "Criminals are just too smart nowadays."

"Not really," Detective Wilson said. "You'd think they would always wear gloves to avoid leaving fingerprints, but many times, criminals forget to cover their hands."

"Not in this case," Zeke said glumly.

Detective Wilson stood up. "I'd better go board up

that window for your aunt." He winked at them. "She promised me an extra-big slice of pie as payment."

Aunt Bee found the twins wiping up the charcoal dust on the kitchen table a few minutes later. "Is that my blush brush?" she asked, peering closely at the table. "And my mortar and pestle? Why is it all black?"

They explained what they'd done and promised to clean everything.

"I should hope so," she said sternly. "Did it work?"

"The fingerprinting worked, but it didn't point to the culprit," Jen explained.

"Maybe if we had the note," Zeke hinted, "we could analyze the handwriting?"

"I don't think so." Aunt Bee dug through her skirt pocket and her hand came out holding a piece of paper, which she placed on the table in front of the twins.

Zeke and Jen stared at it. It was the threatening note, all right, but Aunt Bee wasn't kidding when she'd said they couldn't analyze the handwriting.

"'Leave now or else!'" Jen read. "The letters are all cut from magazines!"

"Anyone could have done this," Zeke added with a groan.

The twins sagged. "Now what are we supposed to do?"

13

Totally Clueless

"Mr. Mitchell!" Zeke exclaimed.

Jen looked at her brother. "What about him? He's gone. I saw him leave."

"Don't you remember all the magazines in his room?"

"That's right!" Jen stopped and thought a moment. "That doesn't make sense, though. Remember, he was with me in the kitchen when someone threw the dumbbell through Mrs. Adams's window." She shook her head doubtfully. "I don't think it could have been Mr. Mitchell, but I suppose we shouldn't totally rule him out, either."

Zeke picked up the note and stared at it as if that would give him answers. "The magazines Aunt Bee keeps in the parlor for the guests! That's it!" He jumped to his feet. "Ouch! I forgot about my twisted ankle." He hobbled out of the kitchen, through the dining room, and into the parlor. "I was straightening these up earlier, and I noticed some cut pages. Look." He flipped through the most recent issue of *B&B Life*. Several pages were neatly cut or missing altogether.

Jen frowned. "But it could have been anyone, since everyone has access to these. Every time we get a good clue, it just leads us back to the beginning."

They flopped on the couch. Woofer ambled over to them and lay his big, hairy head between them.

Jen laughed and tousled the hair in front of Woofer's eyes. "So what now?"

"I guess we should make suspect sheets to try to figure out what's going on."

The twins went to the lighthouse tower for privacy and settled on Jen's bed. They wrote out suspect sheets for each guest.

Mystic Lighthouse

Suspect Sheet

Name: Mrs. Adams

Motive: wants job

Clues: 1. She was almost run off the cliff by a red car. Who did it?

2. SHE DIDN'T WANT TO CALL THE COPS.

3. Why was she snooping around in Dr. Bowles's room?

4. IS SHE THE ONE WHO HID HIS BOX IN THE PARLOR? SHE COULD HAVE SEEN IT WHEN SHE WAS SNOOPING IN HIS ROOM, BUT WHY WOULD SHE WANT IT?

5. DUMBBELL WAS THROWN THROUGH HER WINDOW WITH THE NOTE ATTACHED.

Mystic Lighthouse

Suspect Sheet

Name: DR. BOWLES

Motive: WANTS JOB

Clues: 1. NOT AFRAID OF SNAKES AND HAS A SNAKE RING. COULD HE HAVE PUT THE SNAKE IN MS. HARTLET'S ROOM?

2. Out late and opened side door to sneak snake in?

3. DID HE REALLY FIND MR. CRANE'S BRIEFCASE OR DID HE HIDE IT IN THE BUSHES HIMSELF?

4. What's in his locked box? And why are there strange initials on the box?

5. Too jolly to be believed?

Mystic Lighthouse

Suspect Sheet

Name: Mr. Crane

Motive: wants job

Clues: 1. He was the one to point out only ONE of them would get the job.

2. WHO STOLE HIS BRIEFCASE?

3. Very suspicious phone conversations.

4. Acts nervous, like he might be up to something. Very mean to everyone.

5. HIS ROOM IS UPSTAIRS. COULD HE HAVE PUSHED MR. MITCHELL DOWN THE STAIRS?

6. Was he really talking to his wife about "everyone suspicious" or did he fake the "I love you, too, dear," just to throw us off the track?

Mystic Lighthouse

Suspect Sheet

Name: Ms. Hartlet

Motive: wants job

Clues: 1. Acting very nervous.

2. Her room is upstairs. Could she have pushed Mr. Mitchell down the stairs?

3. She had gloves, so she could have taken the dumbbell without leaving fingerprints. But how did she get into Mr. Mitchell's room?

4. What was in the letter that she got? Why did she tear it up? And why did the part Jen found say, "Do whatever it takes to get the job"? Did that mean hurting or even killing the others to get them out of the way?

Mystic Lighthouse

Suspect Sheet

Name: Mr. Mitchell

Motive: wants job

Clues: 1. Has a dented car!

2. DID HE REALLY GET PUSHED DOWN THE STAIRS? OR DID HE TRIP? OR DID HE FAKE IT?

3. AND WHY WAS HE UPSTAIRS? HE SAID HE WAS LOOKING FOR HIS STOPWATCH. BUT WAS HE JUST SNOOPING AROUND? OR WAS HE UP THERE TO PUT THE SNAKE IN Ms. HARTLET'S ROOM AND SHE JUST DIDN'T SEE IT UNTIL THE NEXT DAY?

4. It was his dumbbell that was thrown through Mrs. Adams's window.

5. LEFT THE SCENE OF ALL THE CRIMES. BUT WHY, IF HE WANTED THE JOB SO MUCH?

Jen snorted with disgust. "This is impossible. We'll never figure out what's going on."

"I know what you mean." Zeke's shoulders slumped. "We must be missing a really important clue."

"What, though?"

"I don't know. But if we could find something, I bet everything else would fall into place."

They sat silently for a minute, then Jen said slowly, "We have to go back to the beginning again—back to Dead Man's Curve."

Zeke gulped. His ankle hardly even twinged anymore, but the thought of what could have happened to him put a rock in his throat. "Aunt Bee won't like it," he said, knowing this wouldn't stop his twin.

"We'll just say we're going to the Quick Stop Mart."

"Okay," Zeke reluctantly agreed. Even though he knew Aunt Bee wouldn't like it if she found out, he knew this was the only way to get to the bottom of things.

Fifteen minutes later, he found himself riding around the first bend of Dead Man's Curve. He rode so far off the side of the road that he almost ran head-first into a pine tree.

"Watch where you're going!" Jen shouted.

They jumped off their bikes and left them in the

ditch before running across the road. With her hands on her hips, Jen looked around. "That's weird," she said.

"What?"

"Where are the skid marks?"

"I noticed that, too," Zeke admitted. "I didn't think it was important, though. Mrs. Adams probably exaggerated her accident. After all, it was just a little fender bender."

"It didn't even dent her fender. It just broke her taillight," Jen pointed out.

Zeke frowned. "You know, I never did find any pieces of the taillight."

"What do you mean?" Jen asked, scouting around.

"We saw the broken taillight on her car, right?"

Jen nodded.

"I didn't find any pieces of it when I was here last time, and you don't see any now, right?"

Jen shook her head.

All of a sudden they heard the roar of an engine and tires screeching as a car barreled around the tight bend of Dead Man's Curve.

"Watch out!" Zeke shouted.

Note to Reader

Have you figured out who is behind all the accidents? It's clear that one of the candidates for the principal's job wants their competition to be scared away. But who?

If you review this case carefully, you'll discover important clues that Jen and Zeke have missed along the way.

Take your time. Carefully review your suspect sheets. When you think you have a solution, read the last chapter to find out if Jen and Zeke can put all the pieces together to solve *The Mystery of Dead Man's Curve*.

Good luck!

Solution

Another
Mystery Solved!

Zeke grabbed Jen's arm and yanked her back to the shoulder of the road near the guardrail. The car raced past on the other side of the road, squealing as it rounded the last turn of Dead Man's Curve. Even as it disappeared from sight, the roar of the motor lingered.

"What did you do that for?" Jen demanded, rubbing her arm where Zeke had grabbed her.

Zeke glared at her. "Only to save your life. Aren't you going to thank me? That maniac driver was trying to kill me again."

Jen's eyes widened. "You mean that was the same car that tried to hit you?"

"I'm positive," Zeke said, nodding.

"But I thought you didn't get a good look at it. How can you be sure?"

"The sound of the motor. There must be a major

hole in that car's muffler to make it so loud. It was definitely the same one."

Jen laughed. She couldn't help it.

He scowled at her. "See if I try to save your life again," he said. When Jen didn't stop laughing, he asked her what was so funny.

"I'll tell you later. I promise," she added as his scowl deepened. "Let's just say that part of this mystery is solved. But that doesn't help with the missing taillight." She looked around at her feet.

"It's as if the accident never happened," Zeke mused out loud.

The twins froze as Zeke's comment sank in. Jen snapped her fingers. "Mrs. Adams's toolbox!"

Zeke knew exactly what his sister was thinking. "A hammer."

"Mrs. Adams broke her own taillight. She faked the accident!" Jen exclaimed.

"She must have pulled over somewhere to smash her own car."

"I've got it," Jen called over her shoulder as she ran across the road and hopped on her bike. "Come on!"

Zeke followed Jen at top speed to the Quick Stop Mart. He winced with each downward pedal on his sore ankle, but he didn't slow down. At the store, they raced inside and Jen headed right for the check-out counter where Stacey's brother, Brian, was waiting on a customer. When the customer left, Jen said, "Hi, Brian. Were you working last Sunday?"

Brian looked at the ceiling a second, then nodded. "Yep. What's up?"

"Do you remember waiting on a really tall lady with bright orange hair?"

"Frizzy, like clown hair?" Brian asked right away.

"Yes!"

"Sure, I remember her. She was a little strange. She asked me for a bag, but when I said I couldn't give one out without a purchase, she bought something just so she could have one."

"A toothbrush and toothpaste?" Zeke asked.

"Something like that," Brian agreed.

The twins looked at each other, their blue eyes flashing with excitement.

Jen started with, "Remember Slinky and how . . ."

". . . she was playing with that piece of red plastic," Zeke finished for her.

"Mrs. Adams put the taillight in the bag and threw it away, but Slinky found it."

"Mrs. Adams faked the whole accident."

"If we can find those pieces of plastic, we can prove it!"

"Hey, what's going on?" Brian interrupted.

"Oh, nothing," Jen said, trying to sound casual even though she was jumping with excitement inside. "By the way," she went on, changing the subject, "were you almost late for work today?"

Brian tried to hush her. "Keep it down. The manager said if I'm late one more time, I'm fired. And I need the money to fix my muffler."

Zeke's mouth dropped open and Jen laughed.

"Do you drive an old green car?" Zeke demanded.

Brian grinned. "Yep. Isn't it great?"

"Great?" Zeke burst out. "You almost killed me. Twice!"

"What are you talking about?"

Jen quickly explained how his squealing tires and broken muffler had startled Zeke at Dead Man's Curve.

"You really thought I'd run you off the cliff?" Brian asked Zeke, looking sheepish. "I admit I was going a little over the speed limit, but my tires are low on air, which is why they squeal. And you know about the muffler now. I'm really sorry I scared you."

"I wasn't scared," Zeke said, straightening his shoulders. "Just—uh—concerned."

"We have to go now," Jen said quickly. She started out of the convenience store, making sure Zeke was right behind her.

When they finally made it back to the B&B, they rode right to the garbage bins. Sure enough, there was Slinky, sitting on a red-white-and-blue-striped bag from the Quick Stop Mart as though she were waiting for them. Jen remembered how Slinky had been playing with it earlier, but she hadn't made the connection. Now she pulled the bag out from under the cat and looked into it. She passed it to Zeke without a word.

Zeke peered into the bag at all the smashed pieces of taillight. There was a slight tear in the side where a couple of pieces of plastic must have slipped out for Slinky to play with. "But why? Why would she fake it?"

Jen snapped her fingers. "All the accidents, of course. She was trying to scare everyone away from the job interviews. But if nothing happened to her, it would look suspicious."

"So she made sure the first accident happened to her," Zeke continued. "That way, when things started happening to the other candidates, she wouldn't look guilty."

"That must be why her dent isn't rusty, but Mr. Mitchell's was. His was from an old accident."

"This is all fitting together now," Zeke said.

After a moment of thought, Jen said, "Mrs. Adams had a coughing fit and asked me to get her a glass of water."

"So?"

"I was cleaning Mr. Mitchell's room at the time! And when I came back to give her the water, she was in her room again. That's when she stole the dumbbell!"

"But what about her fingerprints?"

"She had a handkerchief! I thought it was because she was coughing, but it was probably what she used to pick up the weight."

"Perfect!" Zeke exclaimed. "And remember how I said there shouldn't be that much glass outside her window because the weight was thrown *in* and not *out?*"

Jen nodded. "And you were so surprised when I was right. But I should have been wrong! She must have used the weight, or something else heavy, to break the window from inside her room. Then she broke off pieces of the window and dropped the glass in her room so it wouldn't look suspicious."

"She sure is sneaky."

"But how do we prove it?" Jen asked.

"Fingerprints."

"But there weren't any incriminating prints on the weight," Jen protested.

Zeke pulled the note out of his pocket. "How about this?"

They went inside and set up a fingerprinting lab at the kitchen table, then dusted the note for prints.

It was covered with them.

Zeke groaned. "I just remembered that the note was passed around the room. *Everyone* touched it."

Jen started to say something, but the charcoal dust tickled her nose. Even though she tried to stop it, a giant sneeze erupted, blowing dust everywhere. On her second sneeze, the note fluttered.

"Did you see that?" Jen asked, trying not to sneeze again.

Zeke was brushing the black dust off his shirt. "See what?" he asked grumpily.

"Watch." Jen blew lightly on the note. The letter *E* at the end of ELSE flapped up. Most of the letters were glued securely, but this *E*, the largest letter in the note, was only tacked down at the top.

Realization crashed into Zeke's brain. "Fingerprints!"

Very carefully, they dusted the underside of the *E*. Sure enough, one single print showed up. Zeke lifted it very carefully with a strip of tape and affixed the tape to a clean piece of white paper.

Jen inspected the print. "Are you sure you lifted this smoothly?"

"Of course," Zeke said.

"Then what's this line through the fingertip?" She passed the paper to him for a closer look.

"It looks like a cut or a scar."

"Can you tell which finger it is?"

Zeke shook his head. "It looks smaller than a thumb and bigger than a pinky. But other than that, I have no idea."

Jen picked up a scrap of paper and pretended to cut it out, put a dab of glue on the back, and place it down as though she were going to stick it to another piece of paper. "Did you see that?" she asked her brother when she was done.

"Yes, but what's your point?"

Jen showed him her pointer finger. "It's this finger. And . . ." She held up her hand to stop her brother from interrupting. "And Mrs. Adams has a scar on that exact finger from when she cut herself on the day she arrived. She just showed me yesterday how well it was healing. There's a thin scar across her finger just like this fingerprint!"

"What are you two doing?" Detective Wilson asked, leaning over the table.

The twins jumped.

"We figured out which guest is guilty of causing all the accidents," Zeke announced.

Rushing and interrupting each other, the twins told Detective Wilson the entire story, including all the clues they'd missed at first.

"She must be the one," Jen finished. "But now what do we do?"

Detective Wilson nodded thoughtfully. "You two have done enough. In fact, you've done an excellent job. I'll go talk to her. Stay put. There's no telling how angry she'll get, and she could get dangerous."

Jen and Zeke longed to go with him, but one stern look from under his bushy eyebrows kept them from arguing.

When Detective Wilson didn't return immediately, the twins got restless. First they cleaned up their mess, then they settled in the parlor, straining their ears to hear anything from down the hall.

It seemed as if everyone else knew something was going on. Pretty soon all the guests and even Aunt Bee were sitting in the parlor. At last the retired detective returned.

"She's gone," he said, shaking his head. "She admitted to absolutely everything. You kids hit it right on the nose."

"So she faked her accident," Jen said.

"And did everything else, too. She even pretended to hate snakes and she put the snake in Ms. Hartlet's room."

Ms. Hartlet shuddered. "What a dreadful woman."

Jen and Zeke continued to explain how they figured out Mrs. Adams was the guilty one.

"But," Zeke admitted, "we are still a little confused about some of the things we wrote down on our suspect sheets." He turned to Dr. Bowles. "For example, the first night you were here, you came in late. What were you doing?"

Dr. Bowles smiled sheepishly. "I tend to be a bit forgetful, in case you hadn't noticed. I couldn't remember if I'd turned off my headlights when I'd arrived, so I went outside to look. And before you even ask, I have to admit that I took my pillbox downstairs to sort through my medicine, and I forgot that I left it under my chair. I'm sorry I accused someone of stealing it."

"Your pillbox?" Jen said. "You mean your dragon-carved box is full of pills?"

"I take medication for high blood pressure, high cholesterol, allergies, and migraine headaches. I keep the box locked because my grandkids visit, and I don't want them getting into my pills."

"You have a lot wrong with you!" Jen exclaimed without thinking.

Dr. Bowles laughed. "I sure do. It's all from stress. Now I try to keep a positive outlook. It seems the happier I am, the fewer ailments I have. But I have to admit, it's not easy to be jolly all the time."

Zeke laughed. "That certainly explains a lot. But whose initials are on the box?"

"Those are my mother's. It was her pillbox long ago."

Jen turned to Ms. Hartlet.

Ms. Hartlet opened her eyes wide and said, "Surely I wasn't a suspect, too?"

"We did wonder about that letter you got," Jen admitted. "I found a piece of it that said you should get the job no matter what."

Ms. Hartlet laughed. "Oh, that was from my twenty-year-old nephew. He's always bullying me into trying something new. He thought I might purposely not try hard on the interviews. He thinks I should move up in my career, but he also thinks I'm too set in my ways. Too chicken, is how he puts it. He was just urging me to try my hardest to get the job."

Jen laughed. "Well, what about the gloves in your room?"

Ms. Hartlet looked confused as to why the gloves would make her look guilty.

"It's too warm out for gloves," Jen explained, "and if you're wearing gloves, you don't leave fingerprints. So I thought—"

"Those are my lucky gloves," Ms. Hartlet interrupted, laughing. "They belonged to my grandmother.

I bring them to all important events. Kind of like a lucky coin or a rabbit's foot."

Jen groaned. "Boy, anything can look suspicious!"

"Which is why I was a suspect, too, I suppose?" Mr. Crane asked dryly.

"We didn't mean to eavesdrop," Jen said, crossing her fingers behind her back.

"As I already told you," Mr. Crane snapped, "I was talking to my wife."

Jen and Zeke looked at each other and shrugged. They knew it wouldn't do any good to mention all the suspicious things they had heard him say. And anyway, they'd already found the guilty person.

Just then the phone rang. The call was for Ms. Hartlet, and she went to the front desk to talk.

Aunt Bee sighed. "I'm so relieved all this is cleared up. I was afraid we had a poltergeist at work in the B&B."

"It would be cool to have a ghost," Jen said.

"Cool until you came face-to-ghostly-face with it," Zeke teased.

Ms. Hartlet returned, a stunned look on her face.

Aunt Bee jumped to her feet. "What's wrong?"

Shaking her head, Ms. Hartlet said, "Nothing. I— I got the job! The superintendent of schools said they didn't need to do any more interviews because the hiring committee had already agreed that I should be offered the position." She looked apologetically at Mr. Crane and Dr. Bowles. "I'm so sorry."

Dr. Bowles laughed. "Sorry? Don't be silly. I'm sure you'll make a wonderful principal here in Mystic. To tell you the truth, I'm not sure my heart could take all the excitement around here."

Someone in the corner started to laugh. It was not a familiar sound.

Jen gasped. Mr. Crane was laughing so hard that tears were spilling from his eyes. At first she thought he was hysterical with disappointment.

"I'll be fine," Mr. Crane said through his laughter and tears. "I am just so relieved!"

"Relieved?" everyone repeated in unison.

Mr. Crane stretched his arms above his head, looking more relaxed than Jen thought he ever could have. He began to explain. "I love my job. I'm a principal at a small middle school where we have wonderful students. But my wife wanted to move and thought I should have a more prominent position. I love her dearly, but my wife can be a bit pushy." He laughed again.

Jen could hardly believe how sweet he looked when he smiled.

He turned to the twins. "I really was talking to my

wife when you *accidentally* overheard me. I kept telling her how nice the other candidates were and how I'd never be able to compete at the interviews. It all must have sounded rather sinister to you two."

Jen and Zeke grinned. "It sure did!"

"I'm sorry I've been rather, uh, cranky. I don't do well at all under extreme pressure."

"Oh," Ms. Hartlet said, still beaming, "I should probably tell you all what else they said on the phone. The superintendent asked to speak to Mrs. Adams. When I told him she had left, he said the strangest thing. He said that Mrs. Adams had forged some of her letters of recommendation and, in fact, had been fired from her last job! That must be why she was so desperate to scare everyone else away from the job. She knew she didn't have any chance of getting it otherwise."

Slinky slipped into the room then, her fluffy tail waving proudly. Instead of climbing on Woofer, who was sleeping at the twins' feet, she crawled under the sofa and backed out with a cord between her teeth.

Jen squatted down and took the string from her and pulled. The rest of the object appeared. "Mr. Mitchell's stopwatch!"

Zeke laughed. "Another mystery solved!"

About the Author

Laura E. Williams has written more than twenty-five books for children, her most recent being *ABC Kids* and *The Executioner's Daughter*. In her spare time, she enjoys stamping, painting, and photography.

Ms. Williams loves a good mystery. And learning how to lift fingerprints will come in handy when she has to figure out which of her two kids opened the new box of cookies!

Mystic Lighthouse

Suspect Sheet

Name:

Motive:

Clues: